The MAGICAL LAND of BIRTHDAYS

FROM THE CREATOR OF FLOUR SHOP

by

A M I R A H   K A S S E M

illustrations by

E L I S A   C H A V A R R I

AMULET BOOKS

NEW YORK

The Library of Congress has cataloged the hardcover edition as follows:

Names: Kassem, Amirah, author.
Title: The Magical Land of Birthdays : a Flour Shop kids adventure / Amirah Kassem.
Description: New York : Amulet Books, 2019. | Summary: After receiving a magical cookbook and baking her special birthday cake, a young Mexican girl is transported to the Magical Land of Birthdays, where she meets three children from different corners of the world who are also about to turn eleven.
Identifiers: LCCN 2019033762 | ISBN 9781419737435 (hardcover) | ISBN 9781683355762 (ebook)
Subjects: CYAC: Birthdays—Fiction. | Magic—Fiction. | Adventure and adventurers—Fiction.
Classification: LCC PZ7.1.K3715 Mag 2019 | DDC [Fic]—dc23

Paperback ISBN 978-1-4197-3744-2

Text copyright © 2019 Amirah Kassem
Book design by Hana Anouk Nakamura
Flour Shop branding by TPD Design House

Amulet Books are available at special discounts when purchased in quantity for premiums and promotions as well as fundraising or educational use. Special editions can also be created to specification. For details, contact specialsales@abramsbooks.com or the address below.

Amulet Books® is a registered trademark of Harry N. Abrams, Inc.

ABRAMS The Art of Books
195 Broadway, New York, NY 10007
abramsbooks.com

To everyone with a birthday!

*Here's to wishing you find your B-Buds and
spread joy one sprinkle at a time!*

*Keep believing in the magic of birthdays and friendship—
a pocket of sprinkles can change the world!*

AMIRAH KASSEM

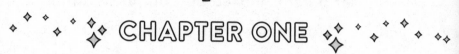

CHAPTER ONE

"HAPPY NEW YEAR!" Amirah sang out.

Her parents looked up from their morning coffee. "Happy New Year, princess," Baba said.

"You're starting the new year off in a good mood," Mama added.

"Well, you know what January first means," Amirah replied.

Mama pretended to look confused. "The first day of the new year?" she teased Amirah.

"No!" Amirah replied with a laugh. "Well, yes! But it means my birthday is in one week. Just one more week to go until I turn eleven!"

"Oh, of course!" Mama replied. "How could I have forgotten?"

Amirah and Mama exchanged a big grin. They both knew that she hadn't forgotten—not for a minute. Birthdays were a very big deal in Amirah's family—and Amirah wouldn't want it to be any other way. All year long, she looked forward to her birthday on January 8. Not just because of the presents or the delicious cake—

though she definitely loved those parts of her birthday. No, the very best thing about her birthday was that it gave Amirah the chance to celebrate with all her favorite people. She invited everybody in her small town in Mexico to her birthday party every year, from her friends to her neighbors to the principal of her school!

"Want some chocolate con leche?" Mama asked as she stood up and walked toward the kitchen. "Your brother will be awake soon and I know he'll want some."

"Yes, please," Amirah said. The warm, sweet drink was one of her favorites, especially at breakfast time. It was a traditional beverage in her country, but Amirah always liked to add an unusual ingredient: a smattering of sprinkles from the container she kept in her pocket. No matter where she went or what she did, Amirah made sure to carry some sprinkles with her. She was a firm believer in the power of sprinkles and their ability to make magic happen just about anywhere.

While Mama measured out the ingredients for chocolate con leche, Amirah walked over to the little desk in the corner of the living room where she kept all her favorite art supplies.

"How are the invitations coming?" Baba asked as he sipped his coffee.

"Almost done," Amirah replied. "Mrs. Maria's will be the first one I deliver. I'm bringing it to her later."

"I'm sure she will like that," Baba said. "I know your visits brighten her whole day."

"I hope so," Amirah said, reaching for her favorite pink glitter pen. Making personalized invitations for her party guests was one of her special traditions, and Amirah had been spending a lot of time at her desk over the last few weeks as she worked on them. Amirah had spent twice as much time on Mrs. Maria's invitation as all the rest. Mrs. Maria, one of Amirah's elderly neighbors and a close friend, treasured the handmade invitations that Amirah had brought her over the years. She kept them on display year-round!

"Oh good, the paint's dry!" Amirah exclaimed. Mrs. Maria's card had a birthday cake on it, covered in colorful sprinkles, of course. A single candle in the cake burned brightly with a flame made from red, orange, and gold glitter.

Amirah carefully tucked Mrs. Maria's invitation into the last envelope and added a handful of shiny confetti. She loved birthdays so much that she even wanted her invitations to feel like a party when her friends and family opened them!

Amirah could tell from the delicious smell of chocolate wafting from the kitchen that her drink was almost ready, so she wandered into the kitchen and sat down at the table.

"Your invitations turned out beautifully this year," Mama said as she stirred the pot of chocolate con leche on the stove. "I noticed you painted a lot of birthday cakes. Any ideas about *your* birthday cake?"

Amirah sighed and shook her head. "I don't know why I can't decide," she replied. "I want it to be delicious—and different—but beyond that, I'm just not sure."

"Try not to worry, princess," Mama said. "You still have a whole week to figure it out. I know the perfect cake will come to you!"

Amirah hoped so. She had already worked out all the other details for her party, from the type of piñata she was going to have (unicorn shaped) to the outfit she was going to wear (rainbow striped dress, denim jacket, and silver glitter sneakers). The candy bags Amirah would hand out to all her guests were even planned out! Every little detail had been finalized, except for the cake.

After breakfast, Amirah spent the next few hours working on the last batch of party invitations. Finally, when they were all finished, she left them to dry on her desk. She grabbed her backpack and her pink sweater and hurried down the path to the sidewalk. Her neighbor Mrs. Maria lived just two doors down. Mrs. Maria's grandkids all lived in the United States, so she treated Amirah like an unofficial granddaughter. Amirah didn't mind one bit. She loved to visit her for an afternoon of stories and conchas. The sweet, seashell-shaped treats were more of a breakfast food, but Amirah loved that Mrs. Maria liked to serve them in the afternoon too!

As she stood on the doorstep, Amirah knocked on the door—*rap-rap-thud-thud-tap-tap!* The special knock was a code to tell Mrs. Maria that she'd come to visit. And sure enough, Mrs. Maria swung open the door just moments later. Her bright smile smoothed out all the lines in her face.

"Happy New Year, Amirah!" Mrs. Maria exclaimed, holding open the door for her.

"Happy New Year!" Amirah replied. "I have something for you!"

Mrs. Maria's eyes sparkled. "Is this what I think it is?" she asked as Amirah handed her the envelope. "Oh good, I was hoping to get one this year!"

"You'll get one every year!" Amirah said with a laugh. Then her eyes widened as she realized that Mrs. Maria's gray hair had a little something extra in it—a lacy cobweb! Luckily, there were no spiders to be seen, and Mrs. Maria laughed as Amirah brushed the cobweb away.

"I've been tidying my attic," she explained. "I always like to begin the New Year with a fresh start. And that includes the house too."

Amirah thought about the clutter under her bed and knew she should follow Mrs. Maria's example.

"Come, sit," Mrs. Maria said. "I want to open this invitation properly, with a nice cup of horchata. And I don't suppose I could interest you in some?"

"Always!" Amirah replied.

Mrs. Maria bustled off to the kitchen and soon returned with a pitcher of cold, creamy horchata and—Amirah grinned—a plate of conchas. As she poured the horchata, a frown flickered across Mrs. Maria's face. She shook her head.

"Ay, me. Something is missing." She sighed. "What would make this food even more festive?"

Amirah raised an eyebrow. "Are you thinking of something . . . colorful? And sweet?"

"Sí, sí, that's exactly it!" Mrs. Maria replied.

"I have just the thing," Amirah said as she pulled the sprinkles out of her pocket. Ever since Mrs. Maria had discovered that Amirah always carried sprinkles with her, she found a way to ask for them whenever they shared a snack or a meal.

"Wonderful! You are ready for anything!" Mrs. Maria said.

Once their cups of horchata were topped

with a rainbow of sprinkles, Mrs. Maria opened the envelope and carefully pulled out the invitation that Amirah had made. As soon as she opened it, shiny bits of confetti fluttered through the air.

"Oh!" Mrs. Maria exclaimed, clapping her hands in delight. "Even the invitation feels like a party!"

"Well," Amirah said, "you know how I feel about birthdays."

Mrs. Maria laughed. "The whole town knows how you feel about birthdays," she replied. "It's a gift, you know. To remember the joy of your special day and carry it in your heart all year long."

"Doesn't everybody feel that way about birthdays, though?" Amirah asked.

"I'm not sure that everyone does," Mrs. Maria replied. Her face broke into a smile as she reached across the table to give Amirah's hand a gentle squeeze. "But lucky for everyone who

has ever met you, you are a wonderful reminder of just how special birthdays are!"

Amirah grinned back at Mrs. Maria.

"Now, this cake you painted," Mrs. Maria continued. "Is this a hint about your birthday cake, eh?"

"You know I can't tell you!" Amirah replied. "It's a secret until the party!" *And so far, it's a secret even from me,* she thought—but didn't say.

Then Amirah noticed a stack of books on the table. "What are all these?" she asked.

"My old cookbooks," Mrs. Maria said. "I'm getting rid of them, once and for all."

Amirah looked up in surprise. "You are? Why?" she said.

"Because I have been cooking for so long, I keep all my favorite recipes up here," Mrs. Maria said, tapping her temple. "I haven't even opened those cookbooks in ages! Some I never even touched, they were just things I picked up through the years."

"You just 'picked them up through the years'?" Amirah repeated, confused.

"Yes, exactly," Mrs. Maria laughed. "I would buy secondhand cookbooks at yard sales or flea markets, or friends would give them to me as gifts. When you like to cook as much as I do, for as long as I have, you just accumulate a collection of cookbooks and you don't even know how!" Mrs. Maria took a final sip of her horchata. "You can help yourself if you want any of them."

"Wow, really?" Amirah asked.

"Sí! Take as many as you want," Mrs. Maria said. "They served me well when I was young like you. Now, if you don't mind, I'm going to start making some pozole for my supper. And you know what? I think I'll make a little extra. Then you can take some home and surprise your sweet mother. Tada! Dinner is ready!"

"She'll love it," Amirah replied. "And so will I!"

Mrs. Maria's cooking was legendary in their neighborhood. Like Mrs. Maria, Amirah's mother was also an outstanding cook and baker, and she never seemed to need a recipe either. Somehow, Mama just knew what a particular dish needed . . . a pinch of this, a spoonful of that. Amirah longed to be so skilled in the kitchen, but she'd never been bold enough to cook without a recipe before.

Maybe if I use Mrs. Maria's cookbooks, I'll learn all her recipes, Amirah thought to herself. She carefully sorted through the stack of cookbooks. There were cookbooks for dinner parties and cookbooks for holidays; cookbooks for everyday meals and cookbooks for special occasions. Amirah's mouth started to water as she flipped through the books. From the kitchen, the delicious smells of sizzling onions and chilies wafted through the dining room as Mrs. Maria prepared a big pot of pozole.

Amirah's fingers brushed against a slim

cookbook. A strange sensation—almost like a spark—tingled up her arm. She paused. Then she picked up the book.

Amirah could tell right away that the cookbook was old. The cover had begun to peel, shedding shimmery gold flakes on her palms. The title, though, blazed as brightly as if it had just been printed. It read:

THE POWER OF SPRINKLES

Amirah's eyes grew wide. *The Power of Sprinkles?* she thought in surprise. She believed in the power of sprinkles more than anyone else she knew—in their ability to make just about any dessert taste better, or to turn even the gloomiest afternoon into a cheerful party. And now, she was holding a whole cookbook that followed the same philosophy?

Well, there was no doubt about it.

That cookbook was meant for her!

Amirah was even more convinced that it was a very special cookbook when she realized every single recipe was for a delicious-sounding cake. Amirah loved cooking, but *baking* was her true passion because she got to use her imagination every time she decorated a cake. Each recipe in this cookbook sounded so delectable that Amirah wanted to make them all. And as far as she could tell, it was the only cookbook in the entire pile that contained recipes for desserts only. Somehow that made it feel even more special.

Amirah slipped *The Power of Sprinkles* into her backpack and stood up. She was just about to ask Mrs. Maria where she had gotten that particular cookbook when a loud *clang* from the kitchen made her jump.

"Mrs. Maria!" she called out as she ran into the kitchen. "Are you okay?"

"Sí, sí," Mrs. Maria replied. "I'm fine. I just dropped the ladle. Luckily it hit the floor instead of my foot! It made a little bit of a mess, though!"

Amirah immediately grabbed a wad of paper towels from the counter to clean up the splatters from the floor so Mrs. Maria wouldn't have to bend down.

"Do you need some help?" Amirah asked after the mess was all cleaned up. "I've always wanted to learn how to make your pozole. It's so good that we never have any leftovers."

Mrs. Maria smiled and made room for Amirah behind the counter. "That's the highest praise a humble cook like me could ask for," she said. "Now, I'll tell you a little secret about my pozole. It's all in the seasoning. Watch how I crumble this oregano . . ."

CHAPTER TWO

THE POWER OF SPRINKLES

THAT NIGHT, Amirah was so engrossed in *The Power of Sprinkles* that she didn't even hear the tap-tap-tap on her bedroom door.

"Amirah?" Mama's voice sounded muffled. "Are you in there?"

"Sí, Mama!" Amirah replied. "Come in!"

"What are you reading?" Mama asked as she sat down on the end of Amirah's bed.

"Mrs. Maria had a bunch of old cookbooks that she doesn't need anymore," Amirah explained. "She said I could help myself to them and when I saw this one . . . well, I felt like it was meant for me!"

"*The Power of Sprinkles*?" Mama said. Her eyes twinkled. "Are you sure you didn't *write* this one?"

"Yes—but I wish I did!" Amirah replied. "Look, there are recipes for all different types of birthday cakes—Mei's Birthday Cake and Ziggy's Birthday Cake and Elvis's Birthday

Cake and on and on. Every single cake sounds amazing. I want to try them all!"

"Reading cookbooks has the same effect on me," Mama replied. Amirah scooted over in the bed to make room for Mama so they could flip through the book together. The pages of the old cookbook were stained and tattered; some even had notes written on them in faint pencil that Amirah could barely read. But she could tell that the notes were not all written in the same handwriting, and that made her wonder who had owned the cookbook before Mrs. Maria. Were any of the notes from Mrs. Maria, or just the previous owners of the cookbook?

Amirah leaned her head against Mama's shoulder as they turned the pages of *The Power of Sprinkles.* Then Amirah saw something that made her sit up straight. For half a second, she almost thought she'd imagined it. Amirah shook her head—blinked—

She hadn't imagined it. The words were right there, printed clear as day:

AMIRAH'S BIRTHDAY CAKE

"Look!" she exclaimed, pointing at the recipe name.

"My goodness!" Mama said. "How surprising!"

That was the understatement of the year. Amirah's name was Arabic, not Mexican, which meant she never stumbled across it. There were no other Amirahs at school, no characters named Amirah in her favorite books, no key chains or hair clips or T-shirts with AMIRAH printed on them in stores. As far as Amirah knew, she was the only Amirah in the whole country. Normally, that didn't bother her one bit. She loved that her name meant *princess* in Arabic, almost like a secret that only Amirah and her family knew. Now that Amirah saw a recipe that shared her name, though, something stirred deep in her heart. It was a feeling of connection.

Amirah's fingers reached out to touch the page. And then—that spark she'd felt before, that tingle in her fingertips—well, this time she *saw* it.

No, Amirah thought.

It wasn't possible.

Yet as Amirah rested her hand on the page for Amirah's Birthday Cake, she could see it. Not just one spark but dozens—hundreds—of specks of golden light, glittering around her fingers, over her hand, up her arm—

Amirah pulled her hand away from the book and looked urgently at Mama, who was casually glancing at the page. It was obvious that she hadn't noticed a thing.

Amirah's hand inched closer to the page. Once more, the bits of light began to gather at her fingertips—

"Listen to this," Mama was saying as she read

the recipe description. "'The magic is in the sprin-kles. Amirah's Birthday Cake, a unicorn cake baked with plenty of surprises, is truly fit for a princess.'"

Mama paused to smile at Amirah. "Hear that?" she asked. "Magic . . . sprinkles . . . uni-corn . . . surprises . . . *princess!* This really does sound like the perfect cake for you!"

As the golden sparkles danced around Amirah's hand, she suddenly realized some-thing. "Mama! This is it!" she exclaimed. "*This* is my birthday cake!"

"Well, of course it is," Mama teased her. "It says so right there."

"Can we make it? For my birthday?" Amirah asked.

"Of course we can," Mama replied. "No other cake in the world would do!"

Sparkles of joy lit up Amirah's heart as she read all the ingredients aloud so Mama could make a shopping list for their next trip to the grocery store.

"I wish we could bake it tomorrow," Amirah said sleepily.

Mama bent down to kiss Amirah's forehead. "Don't worry," she said. "Your birthday will be here soon enough. Good night, my princess."

When Mama turned out the light, Amirah's bedroom was plunged into darkness—except for the rainbow night-light in the corner. Amirah watched the colors swirl across the night-light. First pink . . . then orange . . . all the way to purple, when the cycle began again.

It was the only light in the room; Amirah's fingers were normal now, without a hint of glittery gold around them. Yet she suspected that if she opened *The Power of Sprinkles* again, those sparks would once more dance across her hands.

Amirah knew that she should get out of bed and put the cookbook with the other books on her shelf. It wouldn't be right to just drop it on the floor. But Amirah was suddenly so tired.

She didn't want to get out of her warm, cozy bed, which was as soft as a giant marshmallow. Instead, she slipped *The Power of Sprinkles* under her rainbow pillow. *It will be safe there,* she thought as another wave of sleepiness washed over her. Amirah couldn't keep her eyes open if she tried. She fell, almost instantaneously, into a deep sleep.

Wait.

Was she asleep?

That night, Amirah didn't just sleep.

She dreamed.

◇ ✦ ◇

AMIRAH STRETCHED her arms high above her head. The golden sunshine felt so good, like the sky was smiling on her. She wasn't exactly sure where she was, but Amirah wasn't worried. This place was safe. It was special.

Amirah took a deep breath. All the delicious smells she could dream of tickled her nose—from sugar to cinnamon to caramel to vanilla. It was like visiting a bakery at dawn, when trays of cakes and cookies and breads were pulled from the oven to cool.

No, the scent in the air was even more specific than that. Amirah inhaled again and realized the air smelled exactly like . . . birthday cake. Delicious, sweet birthday cake.

She soon realized that it wasn't just the aroma carried on the gentle breeze that ruffled her curly hair that made her think of birthdays. The path beneath her feet was not dotted with little stones or leaves, but with confetti. And the colorful flowers that lined the path were actually cake balls!

As she wandered, Amirah started to wonder where everyone was. Surely, she wasn't the only person roaming this mysterious and delicious world? She could hear music—no, not just hear it. She could *see* it! Glittering musical notes danced in the air; she plucked one as it fluttered over her head and realized that it was actually a sugar cookie decorated with sparkling sugar.

Amirah couldn't resist. She popped the cookie in her mouth and closed her eyes in delight as it dissolved into sweetness on her tongue, the musical note ringing through her head with a clear, bright tone.

This is incredible, she marveled. *A cookie you can taste* and *hear!*

Amirah decided to follow the musical notes to see if she could find the musician. She stepped off the path, into the green confetti grass, and started walking. Not too far away, she could see a boy standing on the crest of a hill. He was rocking out on a . . . guitar? As Amirah squinted to try to see better, she realized that the guitar he was playing had a big bite taken out of it! That made her even more curious.

Amirah had taken just a few steps when she saw something unexpected: a caterpillar as big as her arm, crawling through the grass. Not just

any caterpillar, though. It was clearly made of fudgy chocolate cake, with a white chocolate face, tiny chocolate shoes, and candy buttons making a polka-dot pattern along its back. *That caterpillar cake must be someone's birthday cake,* Amirah thought.

"Must find Ziggy!" the caterpillar cake huffed as he passed by. He stopped moving and took a quick look at Amirah. "You're not Ziggy!" he mumbled before scurrying on.

"Wait!" Amirah cried. But the caterpillar cake wobbled and bobbled away, until it disappeared into a tunnel in the cocoa-dirt.

Just then, a flash of color caught Amirah's attention. She turned and saw a graceful girl twirling long, flowing purple party streamers in a field across the way.

Strawberries, Amirah thought as she sniffed the air.

She decided to talk to the girl to find out if she knew anything about where they were. But just as Amirah set off in that direction, she noticed something else.

There was a thick-trunked tree nearby, its branches laden with shiny candy apples. That wasn't all, though. There was a person—a girl—standing under the tree.

At least, Amirah thought it was a girl. It was a little hard to tell; the person shimmered like a shadow, a pale, faded figure that stood in stark contrast to all the vivid colors around her.

What really struck Amirah, though, was the sadness that radiated off the girl. Unlike the girl with the streamers and the boy with the guitar, this girl seemed so weighed down by sorrow that she couldn't shake it off. Even standing at a distance, Amirah could sense it. No. Not sense it. She could feel it, in her very own heart.

No one should feel so sad, Amirah thought. *Especially not here, in this magical place.*

She started walking straight toward the

girl, determined to find a way to make her feel better. Determined to help, however she could.

There was a silvery mist rising from the ground; it snaked around the girl's ankles and spread across the ground like a fast-rising river. It felt cool and shimmery against Amirah's skin; she waved her hands, hoping to clear it away. But the more Amirah moved, the thicker the mist grew, until she couldn't see anything around her—not even the tall candy-apple tree.

"Are you there?" Amirah called to the girl. "Who are you? Please—I'm trying to—"

There was no answer.

Amirah closed her eyes as she tried to figure out what to do next. Would the mist disappear on its own? Or would it grow thicker and thicker, trapping her exactly where she stood?

She never did find out.

With a gasp and a start, Amirah awoke.

What a weird dream, she thought, pressing

her hand over her beating heart. Mrs. Maria often said that dreams were like a window into your heart. Through dreams, you could glimpse your past—and if you were very lucky, dreams would let you peek into the future. But as her dream began to fade into memory, Amirah knew that wasn't possible. Her dream had been too wild and wonderful to ever come true.

CHAPTER THREE

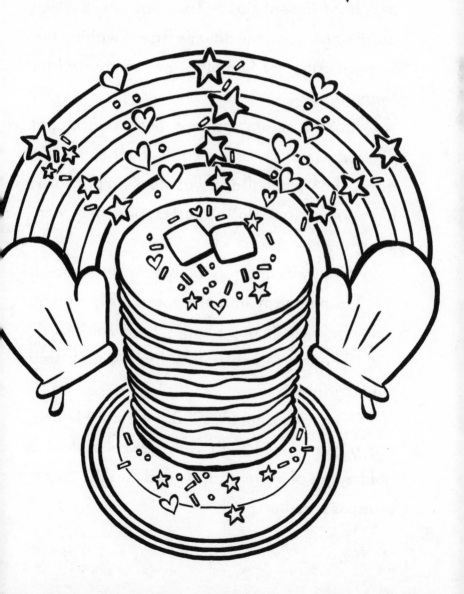

THE NEXT WEEK passed in a blur of last-minute party prep, until one bright, clear morning, Amirah bolted upright in bed. It was here—her birthday—at last! The day she'd been dreaming about, the day she'd been waiting for. She was already beaming, her smile brighter than the sun.

Amirah scrambled out of bed and got dressed as quickly as she could. By the time she got to the kitchen, Baba was stacking pancakes high on a platter. Baba's perfect pancakes were a birthday tradition.

"Happy birthday, princess!" he announced.

Mama swept into the room. "My darling girl!" she cried. "Happy, happy, happy birthday!"

"Thanks, Mama and Baba," Amirah said with a grin.

"Time for pancakes!" Baba said. He held out a plate piled high with pancakes and a golden pat of butter that swirled into the maple syrup as it melted.

"The best birthday breakfast ever," Amirah declared.

"Well, it's a special day," Baba replied. "It's only right that it starts and ends with cakes."

Amirah raised an eyebrow at him. Could pancakes count as cake? Really? Maybe . . . with a few sprinkles . . .

She reached into her pocket and pulled out her container of sprinkles. They rained onto the stack of pancakes, scattering bright specks of color and making her breakfast even more enchanting.

"Oh no! Did I miss out on birthday pancakes?"

Amirah turned in her seat and saw her little brother Amir pad into the kitchen looking very sleepy.

"I might have saved some for you," Amirah replied, her eyes twinkling. "But do you have something to say to me first?"

Amir looked confused for a moment, and

then his face broke into a wide grin. "Happy birthday, Amirah!" he cried.

"Thank you!" Amirah replied. "Just for that I'll share my birthday pancakes with you!" She smiled as her dad set a plate of pancakes down in front of Amir.

As Amirah and her brother devoured the delicious birthday pancakes, Mama was busy arranging ingredients on the counter. Butter . . . eggs . . . flour . . . vanilla . . . and the biggest container of sprinkles Amirah had ever seen.

Baking with Mama was one of Amirah's favorite things in the whole world—and baking on her birthday was even more special. Amirah was already dressed for the occasion, wearing her favorite pink jumpsuit (and sneakers, of course!). Before long, the kitchen was filled with familiar sounds—the crack of eggshells, the whirr of the mixer, Mama's pretty singing, Amirah's laughter. Joy bubbled up and spread throughout the house along with the sweet scent of sugar and vanilla.

After they placed the cake pans in the oven, Amirah glanced at them nervously. Mama didn't bother to set the timer—amazingly, she never needed to use it—but Amirah couldn't help worrying a little. What if her special birthday cake was a flop? After all, it was an untested recipe from a cookbook they'd never used before . . . and Amirah wasn't even sure that Mrs. Maria had ever used it either. When she had asked Mrs. Maria about *The Power of Sprinkles*, Mrs. Maria had just shrugged and said she didn't remember having a book by that name. The book, and its recipes, were a total mystery! Amirah knew that anything could happen with her cake.

Even though Amirah didn't say a word, Mama seemed to know what she was thinking. "Let those cakes bake in peace, princess," Mama called from across the room. "That's how the magic happens. Plus, we need to make frosting—lots and lots of frosting."

Amirah knew that Mama was right. "Okay," she said, pushing up her sleeves.

"We'll need a big bowl of white frosting," Mama said, glancing at the recipe. "And for the unicorn's mane—"

"Can I choose the colors?" Amirah asked excitedly.

"Of course you can," Mama replied.

"Then I choose—rainbow!" Amirah announced.

"I had a feeling you might," Mama said, gesturing to six smaller bowls that she'd already lined up on the counter. There was one for each color!

Making an enormous batch of frosting distracted Amirah from her baking worries. She stirred several drops of food coloring into each small bowl, watching as the color of the frosting transformed like magic. Pink, orange, yellow, green, blue, and . . . purple. Sort of. Almost perfect. Amirah wrinkled her nose as she looked closely at the bowl with the purple frosting. The color was beautiful, but it wasn't exactly the right hue. Biting her lip, Amirah added two more drops of red coloring to the bowl and stirred it . . . and then the perfect shade of purple bloomed in the bowl. Amirah grinned as she looked at the vibrant rainbow of colors before her.

The next thing she knew, Mama was opening the oven door.

"Just right," Mama said, smiling at the golden yellow cakes as she pulled each pan from the oven.

Amirah closed her eyes and breathed in deeply. The delicate scent of vanilla filled the air, and she could tell just from the smell that her unicorn birthday cake was going to be unbelievably delicious!

After the cakes cooled, Amirah and her mother began to assemble them. First, they used a round cookie cutter to make a hole right in the center of each layer except the top one, which they set aside. Then they stacked the cake layers, one on top of the other, using sweet, sticky frosting to hold them together.

Mama pushed the massive container of sprinkles over to Amirah. "Would you like to do the honors?" she asked.

"You know it!" Amirah exclaimed. With the holes in the cake layers carefully positioned, there was a secret hollow inside, just waiting to be filled with sprinkles. From the outside, no one would be able to tell. But once they sliced open the cake that night . . . well, just thinking about how surprised everyone would be by the cascade of sprinkles made Amirah shiver with excitement.

Amirah concentrated hard as she got ready to pour the sprinkles into the cake. One mistake, and they could spill all over the counter, tumbling down to the floor. The last thing Amirah wanted to do was waste something as special as sprinkles!

In the quiet kitchen, Amirah and Mama could both hear the soft rustle as the sprinkles poured into the cake hollow. Amirah needed to use almost the entire container to fill up the cake. Luckily, only a few sprinkles bounced off the top of the cake and landed on the counter.

"Perfect," Mama declared. "Now for the top layer . . ."

As Amirah placed the final layer on the very top, she realized she was holding her breath.

"Phew!" Mama said as Amirah carefully positioned the top layer of the cake. "That's one tall cake!"

"Just wait until we add the unicorn's horn," Amirah said, giggling. She'd already covered an ice cream cone with edible gold dust to make it glimmer like magic.

"First things first," Mama replied. "Frosting, unicorn ears, unicorn eyes—"

"And don't forget the mane!" Amirah reminded her.

Mama and Amirah joked and laughed as they spread a thick layer of creamy white frosting over the cake, concealing all the layers. Then they gave the unicorn two pointy ears, made of white chocolate, and black eyes, one of them winking. Amirah's favorite part was using different pastry tips to swirl frosting into a curly mane that cascaded around the unicorn's head.

Then, the final step: placing the unicorn's golden horn right in the middle of its forehead.

"Does it . . . does it look okay?" Amirah asked Mama.

"It looks *incredible!*" Mama exclaimed. "I'm going to get my phone. We need to take some pictures of this masterpiece!"

Alone in the kitchen, Amirah stared at the unicorn cake. It looked so delicious—and those breakfast pancakes suddenly seemed like hours ago. What she wouldn't give for a taste of her special cake . . . not even a whole bite, just a nibble, like a sneak preview . . .

Of course she couldn't do that, though. Of course it was impossible. The unicorn cake had to be utterly perfect for everyone who would be at her party tonight. Amirah knew she would just have to wait.

Or would she?

There were cake crumbs left in the pans.

Smears of frosting in the bowls.

And a smattering of sprinkles on the countertop.

Amirah smiled to herself. She wouldn't have to cut into the unicorn cake to taste it after all!

She moved quickly, pressing her thumb into the crumbs, then scraping some frosting out of the bowl. Finally, she added a few sprinkles on top.

Then she licked them up!

Amirah didn't think it would be possible for that gorgeous cake to taste even better than it looked, but somehow it did. She had never tasted anything like it before. It was sweet but not too sweet, butter and sugar and vanilla coming together in perfect harmony. The fluffy cake . . . the sugary frosting . . . the sprinkles dancing on her tongue . . .

Suddenly the colors in the room were falling away. Streaks of them, brighter and brighter, like the tail of a shooting star, like a firework glittering through the darkness. Amirah felt herself tumbling, over and over, as though she were falling, falling, falling through a cascade of colorful sprinkles until she landed with a gentle plop on a soft surface . . .

She blinked.

How did she get outside?

Wait—*was* she outside?

She sat up in the grass—no, not grass, something else, something soft and bright green like grass, but it was . . .

Confetti? Amirah thought.

Slowly, the world came into focus; the mosaic of sprinkles shifted as they arranged themselves into patterns. Their edges blurred together into a crystal blue sky with puffy cotton candy clouds . . . rolling meadows of grass-green buttercream frosting dotted with colorful cake ball flowers . . .

"I know this place," Amirah whispered. She'd seen it before, in her dream. In the distance, she heard a song . . . and that was familiar too.

Whizzzzzzzz!

Amirah ducked as something zipped past her head—

Whizzzzzzzz!

And again—

Whizzzzzzzz!

And again!

CHAPTER FOUR

AMIRAH DROPPED TO the ground and waited to see if anything else was going to zoom through the air toward her head. All she could hear was the sound of her heartbeat thundering in her ears.

That's when Amirah realized that the music, wherever it was coming from, had stopped.

"Are you okay?"

Amirah looked up to see a boy running toward her. There was a note of urgency in his voice, as if he'd seen her sudden nosedive. He held out a hand to Amirah and helped her to her feet.

"Thanks," she said. "What *were* those things? I didn't get a good look."

The boy smiled sheepishly. "They were, uh, musical notes," he said. "I found this cake guitar and first I kind of took a bite—it was *delicious*—and then I wondered if maybe I could play a song. I was jamming on it and the next thing I knew, these musical notes made of cookies were flying into the air! And then I got a little carried away and I guess the musical notes did too. Sorry about that!"

"Don't worry about it," Amirah replied. "Your song was cool."

"I've played a lot of guitars before, but I've never seen anything like that," the boy continued, shaking his head in astonishment.

As the sunlight glinted off his hair, Amirah tilted her head and looked at him. He seemed so familiar, but she definitely didn't know him from home.

Suddenly, Amirah gasped. "I know you!" she exclaimed. "You were in my dream!"

"Your dream?" the boy repeated.

"Yes! I dreamed about this place the other night!" she cried. "And you were there!"

"You look familiar to me too," the boy said. "I wonder if—"

"Did you dream about this place?" Amirah asked eagerly.

The boy shrugged. "I don't know. I never remember my dreams."

Amirah's intuition tingled. She couldn't explain why, but she felt sure that he had dreamed about this place, just as she had.

"By the way, I'm Elvis," the boy said.

"Elvis? Like the musician?" Amirah asked.

"That's who my parents named me after," the boy replied, his face lighting up in a proud grin. "Which is cool since I'm a musician too!" Elvis paused and his cheeks flushed a bit and Amirah noticed he suddenly looked unsure of himself. "I mean, I love music and I *want* to be a musician. Maybe someday I'll be a professional . . . but until then, all I can do is practice."

"My name is Amirah," Amirah replied. "And I say, if you *love* music and you *play* music, then you *are* a musician!"

Elvis grinned shyly, the unsure expression slowly fading from his face. "Sounds good to

me! So yeah, I *am* a musician! What about you, Amirah?"

"Hmmm . . ." Amirah chewed her lip as she considered the question. "I love to bake, so I'm a baker! And I love dancing, so I guess I am a dancer too . . ." Her voice trailed off, and she shrugged. "I like all sorts of things! I definitely like music too. It's so cool that you are a musician!"

Elvis nodded as the grin on his face grew wider. Amirah had a feeling they were going to be fast friends.

"Do you know where we are?" Amirah asked a moment later.

"No idea," Elvis said as he looked around. "But I like it!"

"Me too," Amirah said. "Should we— explore a little?"

"Sure," Elvis said. "Though I don't know how to top a guitar made of cake."

"Try frosting," Amirah joked.

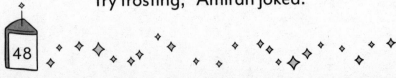

It took Elvis a second to get it, but when he did, he burst out laughing. "Good one," he said.

They cut through the meadow to a path paved with sprinkles. Amirah absentmindedly reached into her pocket and wrapped her fingers around the small container of sprinkles, relieved that it hadn't fallen from her pocket when she'd been transported here. She had a feeling it might come in handy.

The path made a sharp turn, and as they rounded the curve, Amirah noticed a field of giant strawberries. The scent of sun-warmed berries filled the air. It smelled so delicious that Amirah couldn't help breathing in so deeply that she made herself a little dizzy.

And there was a girl, right in the middle of the field, bouncing up and down on the giant strawberries. She was somersaulting high into the air without a care in the world. In her hand she held a long purple streamer that flitted and fluttered through the air. Her short, glossy black hair was pulled into two pigtails that bobbed along with her every movement.

"Look at her go," Elvis cried, pointing to the girl. "It's like she's dancing in a bouncy house strawberry field!"

"I know her," Amirah whispered.

"From your dream?" he asked.

Amirah nodded. She couldn't wait to meet this girl, but at the same time, she hated to interrupt her. The girl danced and bounced with such grace and ease that she looked like a gymnast and a ballerina combined.

It turned out that Amirah didn't need to interrupt her after all. At that moment, the girl glanced over. She definitely noticed Amirah and Elvis, but she continued her routine to the very end of the field, where she somersaulted and landed right in front of them.

"Hi! I'm Mei," she said, waving. "Are you visiting too?"

Amirah and Elvis exchanged a glance, then

introduced themselves. "Um . . . I guess we're visiting," Amirah told Mei. "Though I don't really know where we are."

"I don't either, but I love it here," Mei announced. "It's not like anywhere I've been in Japan before."

"Is that where you're from?" Amirah asked her.

Mei nodded.

"Wow," Amirah replied. "I'm from Mexico."

"Is that where we are?" Mei asked.

"No, I don't think so," Amirah said.

"Well, I'm from the United States, and we definitely aren't there," Elvis spoke up.

"So your routine was pretty amazing," Amirah said a few moments later. "You are such a good gymnast!"

"Thank you!" Mei exclaimed. "I love gymnastics! It's my thing!" Mei bounced on her toes in excitement. "What about you? What are you both into?"

"Oh, I love to bake," Amirah replied. "And dance . . . and I have a ton of hobbies actually! Elvis over here . . ." Amirah looked at Elvis and gave him an encouraging smile.

"I'm a musician," Elvis said finally.

"That's so cool." Mei nodded. "Nice to meet both of you!"

Just then, a swarm of shimmery butterflies fluttered up from the field. As they flew overhead, they dusted Amirah, Mei, and Elvis with a sprinkling of glitter.

Amirah laughed with glee. "This is the coolest birthday ever!" she exclaimed.

Mei and Elvis turned to her, wearing matching expressions. Amirah couldn't quite name it . . . they looked surprised, or stunned, or maybe even shocked.

"Today is your birthday?" Elvis asked slowly.

Amirah nodded.

"But it's *my* birthday!" Mei exclaimed. A wide smile of delight crossed her face. "Wow!

52

I've never met anyone with my birthday before. That makes us birthday twins!"

"Triplets," Elvis said.

"Wait a second," Amirah said. "You mean it's *your* birthday too?"

Elvis, grinning, nodded.

"This *can't* be a coincidence!" Amirah said. "I mean, what are the odds that the three of us all end up in this fantastic land—and we all just happen to have the same birthday?"

"Happy birthday, by the way," Elvis said.

"Happy birthday!" Amirah and Mei replied at the same time.

"We're the Birthday Buds," Amirah declared. "The B-Buds!"

"B-Buds," Mei repeated. "I like it. I like it a lot."

"Happy birthday, B-Buds!" Elvis sang, pretending to play an air guitar.

"What are you doing to celebrate back home?" Amirah asked. "My mom and I made the most incredible cake this morning. It's shaped like a unicorn, with all these rainbow frosting swirls for the mane and a shimmery golden horn, and inside . . . well, you kind of have to see it to believe it, but inside there's a special surprise!"

"That sounds amazing," Mei replied. "I have a special cake too. My oba-chan makes it every year! It's a strawberry shortcake, made of sponge—"

"Sponge?" Elvis asked, wrinkling his nose.

"Sponge *cake*," Amirah explained. Then she glanced over at Mei. "Right?"

"Exactly right," Mei replied. "Oba-chan brushes it with sugar syrup and layers it with fresh whipped cream and the most beautiful strawberries you can imagine!"

"Like those, I bet," Amirah said as she gestured at the field.

"Yeah—kind of," Mei said. "The strawberries back home aren't quite so big, though!"

Then she turned to Elvis. "Do you have a special birthday cake?"

"Mmm-hmm. Peanut butter and banana," he said.

"I've never had peanut butter and banana cake before," Amirah said. "Peanut butter and banana sandwiches, yes . . . peanut butter and banana *cake*, no."

"It's soooo good," Elvis told her. "The cake is like banana bread, but fluffier, and the frosting—that's my favorite part—is like really sweet, creamy peanut butter. I could eat it every single day!"

Suddenly, Amirah saw something across the strawberry field, where a lone candy-apple tree grew. She felt that same strange tingly feeling, as if sprinkles were cascading down her spine.

There was a figure, standing alone, watching them.

Amirah's voice dropped to a hush. "Do you see that?" she asked her new friends.

"Is that a person?" Mei asked.

Amirah nodded. "I think it's a girl," she started to say.

Then something incredible happened. The girl—whoever she was—flickered, as though she were made of light that had started to dim. Just as quickly, she appeared solid again. But that flickering—

Amirah was sure she'd seen it, and from the looks on her friends' faces, she knew they'd seen it too.

"I know her!" Amirah said. "I saw her in my dream!"

WITHOUT ANOTHER WORD, Amirah took off running across the strawberry field, weaving through the long rows of plants and even leaping over some of them. She heard footsteps thundering behind her and felt a pulse of gratitude in her heart. She should've known that Elvis and Mei would follow her.

After all, that's what friends are for.

As she got closer, Amirah got a better look at the girl. She had long blond hair that had been twisted into a braid, and she was wearing a sundress that seemed to change colors when she moved. A sense of sadness hung over her like a shadow.

"Hey," Amirah called. "I want to—"

When the girl looked up, their eyes met. Amirah was struck by the sorrow in the girl's gray-green eyes.

"Please . . ." Amirah said breathlessly.

The girl slipped around the other side of

the tree. Amirah caught a glimpse of her dress, flickering—

But by the time she reached the candy-apple tree, the girl was gone.

Amirah leaned against the grooved tree trunk and realized it was made of chocolate. She absentmindedly broke off a piece of chocolate bark and began to nibble at it. So many questions swirled through her head, it was hard to keep track of them all.

"Did you find her?"

Amirah glanced up to see Elvis and Mei standing nearby. She shook her head. "I got pretty close," she replied. "Close enough to look into her eyes. But she . . . disappeared . . ."

"Like . . . vanished?" Mei asked incredulously. "Into thin air?"

"Yes and no," Amirah said. "I mean, I guess it's possible. But she might've run away instead."

"But why?" Elvis asked. "I mean, you're not exactly scary, you know?"

"Thanks." Amirah chuckled. "She definitely didn't want to talk to me. She just . . ."

When Amirah's voice trailed off, Mei nudged her. "What?" she said.

"I don't know." Amirah sighed. "She just seems so . . . so . . . so sad. She seems like she needs a friend."

Everyone was quiet for a long moment.

"It doesn't seem fair that she feels so sad in such an incredible place," Mei finally said.

"I know, right?" Amirah said. "This place is made of pure joy—"

"And sugar!" Elvis cracked.

"Yes, joy and sugar," Amirah said, laughing again. Then a new thought struck her, making her laughter fade away. "Oh no."

"What's wrong?" Elvis asked.

"Do you think it's *her* birthday too?" Amirah asked. "Is she one of the B-Buds?"

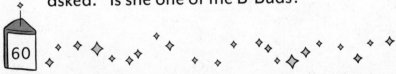

From their silence, Amirah could tell that Elvis and Mei hadn't thought of that either.

"No one should be miserable on their birthday," Mei said firmly. "It should be against the law!"

"I agree," Amirah said. "A birthday is special . . . perfect . . . a day to celebrate being born. Being here!"

"Not just here, though," Elvis said a moment later. "But also being at home."

"Being with family." Mei nodded.

"And being with friends," Amirah added. "Friends. Maybe that's it. Maybe she needs a friend."

"If it's her birthday too, she definitely needs her B-Buds," Mei said.

"Definitely," Amirah agreed. "So that means we have to find her."

"She could be anywhere, though," Elvis said. "Where do we start?"

No one could answer his question. Wherever

they were, the land was big and broad, stretching as far as the eye could see in every direction. Amirah sat down with a sigh and started drumming her fingers on the ground. Should they go back to where she'd started? Forge ahead into the places unknown? Keep following the trail?

Zbp. Zbp. Zbp.

Amirah's fingers stopped moving.

Zbp. Zbp. Zbp.

There was a faint trembling happening under the ground. Amirah could barely hear it— she could barely feel it—but somehow, she knew it was there.

Zbp. Zbp. Zbp.

Amirah leaned closer to the ground, and that's when she saw it: a smattering of sprinkles, vibrating in time with the trembling she sensed. Instinctively, she reached for her little container of sprinkles, just in case she'd accidentally spilled some.

But it was still in her pocket, the lid screwed on tightly as always.

That meant the sprinkles, wherever they'd come from, were part of this place—this mysterious, magical place.

Zbp. Zbp. Zbp.

Amirah tilted her head and squinted as she stared at the sprinkles. They were still moving, yes—but not randomly. It was almost as if they were moving with purpose.

Zbp. Zbp. Zbp.

With every pulse, the sprinkles moved closer together. Closer. Closer.

Amirah didn't realize she was holding her breath until she suddenly gasped.

The sprinkles had formed the letter F, as clear as day.

That wasn't all. The ground was still trembling.

And the sprinkles were still moving.

"Look!" Amirah cried. "A letter! No—it's a-a-a word!"

In a flash, Mei and Elvis knelt on the ground beside her. The three friends sat in expectant silence, watching as the sprinkles shifted, until at last Amirah could see what they were trying to say.

"Find!"

CHAPTER SIX

THE INSTANT AMIRAH said the word, the sprinkles broke apart, scattering to the edge of the clearing. *Oh no!* she thought. What had happened? Had she broken the spell?

"I don't understand," Elvis cried. "Find what?"

"Shhh!" Mei hushed him.

The sprinkles were already moving again.

They inched across the clearing, trembling and twitching, and began to form a new set of letters.

"C," Amirah whispered.

"A," Mei said.

"R," Elvis said.

"A," Amirah said. "Cara!"

Once again, the sprinkles split apart.

"Find Cara," Amirah said. "Who's Cara? Is that the girl's name?"

"Look," Mei cried. "The sprinkles are moving again!"

"T-h-e," Elvis said. "Find Cara the—"

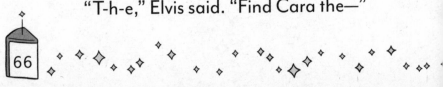

"The what?" Mei asked. "That makes no sense. What does that even mean?"

"I have a feeling," Amirah said as the sprinkles danced into a new formation, "that we're about to find out."

U-N-I-C-O-R-N.

"Find Cara the Unicorn!" Amirah exclaimed.

A sudden gust of air blew through the clearing, lifting the sprinkles up into a cloud of sparkles. They swirled away until even the last sparks had faded from view.

"Find Cara the Unicorn," Amirah said again. She had hoped that the sprinkles would explain everything, but they'd left her feeling only more confused.

"Does that mean that there are *unicorns* here?" Mei asked, her eyes wide.

"I guess so," Amirah said slowly. "I mean, when you think about it, a unicorn wouldn't be the most unusual thing we've seen today. Right?"

Elvis jumped to his feet. "Why are we just sitting around?" he asked. "The sprinkles said we've got to find Cara the Unicorn. So let's go!"

"We need a plan," Mei pointed out. "We can't just run all over the place, like we're on a wild goose chase."

"Or a wild unicorn chase," Amirah said. To be honest, she thought that both her friends were right. But it was impossible to make a plan when they knew so little about this strange and magical place. Should they venture into the shadowy forest? Or continue along the path that had led them to Mei?

"Let's go back to the candy-button path," Amirah finally suggested. "It has to lead somewhere. Maybe if we explore a little, we'll find out more about where we are."

"And maybe we'll even find Cara the Unicorn," Elvis said.

"Or the girl!" Mei added.

The friends hurried out of the strawberry field and back to the path. They began to run together, laughing and shrieking in the warm sunlight as the path twisted and turned. As they ran, Amirah noticed that the candy buttons changed. They became larger and rougher, more uneven. The friends had no choice but to slow down as they crossed the rough terrain.

"So much for the smooth path," Elvis said. "I'm kind of missing those candy buttons."

"Me too," said Amirah. "This feels like hiking in the mountains. You have to watch every step."

Mei's gymnastics training made it easy for her to leap nimbly along the trail. "I think the candy buttons have turned into rock candy," she said.

"It really is a rocky road," Amirah joked. The craggy candies were colorful but almost clear; they glinted in the sunlight as if they were flecked with mica.

Ping!

"Hey! Check it out!" Elvis yelled. The girls turned to watch him hop onto a rock.

Ping!

As Elvis stepped on it, the rock candy lit up and played a musical note.

"Wow!" Amirah exclaimed. She and Mei jumped onto other pieces of rock candy, making the clear, crystal notes ring through the air like a bell. Soon the air was filled with a jumble of musical notes, ringing like wind chimes.

Suddenly, Elvis stopped. He held up his hand. "Did you hear that?" he asked.

"Hear what?" Amirah asked. Of course they'd all heard the jumble of musical notes chiming through the air.

"It sounded like a song," Elvis said.

Mei and Amirah exchanged a glance. Amirah could tell that Mei hadn't heard a song either.

But Elvis was a musician and he loved music more than anything. Maybe he'd heard something the other B-Buds had missed.

"Did . . ." Mei began. Her voice trailed off when she noticed the intense look of concentration on Elvis's face.

"Dah-dah-dah-dah," he hummed under his breath.

Amirah tilted her head and listened carefully. The tune was familiar. She felt certain that she'd heard it before.

"Dah-dah-dah-dah," Elvis hummed again. Then, carefully he leaped from a blue rock candy, to a green one, to a pink, to a purple—

Incredibly, the candies chimed out the exact same notes that Elvis had hummed!

"Wow!" Mei exclaimed.

"How did you *do* that?" Amirah asked.

Elvis grinned and shrugged. "My music teacher says I have a good ear," he replied.

"Can you do it again?" Mei said.

"I think so," he replied. "Actually, I'm going to try to play a whole song."

The girls watched as Elvis jumped from stone to stone. The notes filled the air in a recognizable pattern, a tune that Amirah could almost name. Even cooler, though, was that Elvis's jumps along the rock-candy trail looked like a dance.

Dah-dah-dah-dah-dah-dah

Dah-dah-dah-dah-dah-dah

Dah-dah-dah-dah-dah-dah-dah

Suddenly, Amirah recognized the song— just in time to sing the last line.

"Happy birthday to youuuuuuuuuuu!" she sang out.

"Amazing!" Mei cried as she burst into applause. Amirah started clapping too, and Elvis couldn't hide his pleased smile.

"Show me how," Amirah said.

"Sure," Elvis replied. "Each color of rock

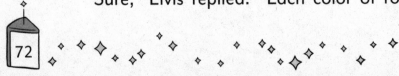

candy represents a different note. So, just like a piano, or a xylophone, if you touch them in a particular order . . ."

"It will play a song," Mei finished for him.

"Exactly. It's really pretty simple," Elvis said. "The right notes, in the right order, and boom— you have a song. Come here, Amirah, and I'll show you how to play 'Happy Birthday.'"

Amirah skipped across the rock candy, making a jumble of notes drift into the air. She soon memorized the pattern of rocks she had to step on to play the familiar tune.

Elvis's eyes twinkled. "Now, if we really want to take it to the next level," he began.

"I'm listening," Amirah replied.

"You could play the melody—that's the part I taught you—and I'll play the harmony," he replied. "A duet!" Then Elvis turned to Mei. "And you can sing," he said.

Mei blushed and put her hands on her cheeks. "Me? Sing? All by myself?" she asked.

"Sure. Why not?" Elvis asked. "You have such a nice speaking voice that I bet you're a great singer."

"But—what if I mess up?" Mei asked. "What if I sing a wrong note? I'd be so embarrassed!"

"Don't be!" Amirah assured her. "We're your friends! Your B-Buds! You never have to feel embarrassed in front of us!"

"Besides, mistakes happen sometimes," Elvis added. "Even in music. It's no big deal. Just keep going to the next note."

"Okay," Mei finally said. "If you're sure . . ."

"On my count," Elvis said. "A one, a two, a one, two, three!"

Amirah concentrated so hard on stepping on the right pieces of rock candy that she didn't even glance at her friends. But she could hear the music they were making—Elvis's harmony complementing the melody she played, and Mei's sweet, strong voice spiraling into the sunshine.

It was the most beautiful rendition of the birthday song Amirah had ever heard.

As the last notes drifted into the air and slowly faded, the three friends were quiet. Then, after a moment of pure silence, they began to cheer.

"That was incredible!" Elvis exclaimed. "What a jam session!"

"Let's do it again!" Amirah said.

But before anyone could move, something incredible happened. A bolt of golden light snaked around the rock candies, lighting each one up in turn, until it zipped into a large hunk of rock candy by the side of the trail. The rock began to glow, lit from deep within.

Then, in a glittering flash of light, it cracked open like an egg!

"Did you see that?" Amirah cried. She raced across the rocks, which played a cacophony of musical notes, to reach the rock. She peered into the crack and gasped in surprise.

There was something inside.

"B-Buds!" she yelled. "Check it out!"

Amirah plunged her hand into the opening, rummaged around . . .

"Be careful," Mei cried. "Those edges look rough!"

"I'm fine," Amirah said, still feeling around. "I thought I saw . . ."

Then, her fingers brushed against something smooth and papery.

Amirah pulled out her hand, which clutched a scroll of paper. Instantly, the crack in the rock sealed up, as though it had never existed.

"It's a message!" she cried, unfurling the scroll. "No—wait—it's a map!"

In a flash of blazing light, letters appeared along the top of the map. They read:

WELCOME TO
THE MAGICAL LAND OF BIRTHDAYS!

CHAPTER SEVEN

"'**WELCOME TO THE** Magical Land of Birthdays,'" Amirah read aloud. "Well, B-Buds, I guess we've finally figured out where we are."

"It makes sense," Elvis said, nodding his head. "I mean, everywhere we look is cake and birthday stuff like streamers and confetti—"

"We played 'Happy Birthday' on the rock-candy trail," Mei added.

"*And* it's our birthdays," Amirah said. "All on the same day. I've never seen anything like this map before. It's practically a work of art."

Amirah wasn't exaggerating. The map was beautiful, with tiny, intricate drawings illuminating each area of the Magical Land of Birthdays. There were rolling hills and craggy mountains, gentle meadows and thriving fields. At the top of the map there were a bunch of buildings clustered together that Amirah thought must represent a city. In the very center was a dense forest that looked like it was made of thousands of trees. The candy-button trail cut through the entire land, and so did a roaring river that cascaded over several small waterfalls and split off into smaller streams. The biggest revelation, though, was that the Magical Land of Birthdays was actually an island, surrounded by ocean on all sides.

Mei's finger hovered over the map. "Look at the path," she said in a hushed voice. "It lights up!"

"Will it tell us where to go?" Amirah wondered. She felt a little silly as she said the words. After all, it was a map, not a person.

Then again, nothing in the Magical Land of Birthdays was quite what it seemed.

"It's worth a try," Elvis said, shrugging. He cleared his throat. "Where will we find Cara the Unicorn?"

The map glittered and gleamed, but nothing else happened. No special path lit up. No trail suddenly appeared.

"I guess we could go back to our original plan of exploring," Amirah said. "But at least this time, we'll be exploring with a map."

"Where would a unicorn be?" Mei asked, still staring at the map.

"It's impossible to guess," Amirah said. "A magical creature, in a magical land . . ."

Amirah racked her brain, trying to remember everything she'd ever read about unicorns. There were so many legends about them. They had magical powers, of course, which made humans so determined to capture them that unicorns had nearly become extinct. They were solitary creatures . . . They liked to be alone . . . They liked to be quiet and peaceful . . .

Amirah pulled the container of sprinkles out of her pocket and munched on a handful. Their sweetness dissolved on her tongue as she continued to think through their options. Should they head deeper into the mountains, toward the woods, or head north, toward the city?"

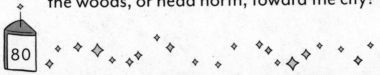

The B-Buds huddled together to look more closely at the map. Amirah pointed to the area on the map that showed the Party Hat Mountains, which would lead them to the Rainbow Forest. Then her finger trailed up to gently tap the area called Sparkle City at the top of the map.

"Rainbow Forest or Sparkle City?" Amirah asked.

"You pick!" Mei said, and Elvis nodded.

"Let's make our way to the Rainbow Forest," Amirah finally said. "We can keep searching for Cara there."

"Sounds like a plan," Elvis replied. "Back down the mountain!"

"Actually," Mei began, "look at this."

Everyone followed her finger as Mei traced a different route, one that climbed the tall mountains and took a shortcut through them.

"What do you see? Is that a passage over the mountains?" Amirah asked.

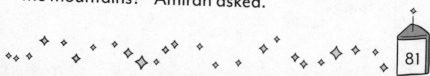

Mei shook her head. "It's a cave that seems to be a tunnel. It's called Candle Cave."

"A tunnel right through the mountains?" Elvis asked.

"Yes," Mei replied. "Yes, look! Candle Cave seems to run through the Party Hat Mountains, just like a tunnel. See how much quicker it will be? We're not too far from the entrance. Then we zip right through the tunnel and climb down the other side of the mountain and we'll be at the forest."

"I get it," Amirah said, nodding her head. "This way, we don't have to go all around the mountain. It really does look like a shortcut. I'm in."

"Me too," Elvis announced.

As the B-Buds stood up, Amirah shook the container of sprinkles. "I almost forgot," she said. "You guys want some?"

"Sure," Mei said, holding out her hand. "Do you, uh, just carry sprinkles with you wherever you go?"

"Absolutely, I do," Amirah said, laughing. "I mean, first, they're delicious."

"You can say that again," Elvis said as he popped a handful into his mouth.

"And second, I just happen to believe that sprinkles make everything better," Amirah continued. "If the weather is gloomy . . . if I'm having a bad day . . . well, I just remember my sprinkles and maybe eat a few and I know it sounds weird, but I feel better instantly. That's the power of sprinkles!"

"I know what you mean. It's not weird," Elvis replied as the trio set off along the path. "Music is kind of like that for me . . . but it's not as easy to carry around in my pocket."

"No, I guess not," Amirah said.

"But you *do* carry music with you," Mei pointed out.

"What do you mean?" he asked.

"Like humming, or snapping your fingers, or drumming on stuff," Mei said.

"I never thought about it like that," Elvis replied.

"What about you, with gymnastics?" Amirah asked Mei. "Do you do little moves all day to keep it with you?"

Mei nodded. "I guess I do, when I can. It's hard for me to sit still all day at school! But mostly I just think about gymnastics a lot. I'll plan routines in my head, or imagine what it would be like to win a medal in the Olympics." Mei paused to hop gracefully over a large rock on the path. "I guess that sounds pretty wild, imagining myself at the Olympics, but it's my biggest dream."

"I think that sounds amazing," Amirah said. "I hope you make it there. I'll cheer for you!"

"Me too!" Elvis added.

Finally, they reached a shadowy opening in the mountain. It was so dark inside that Amirah couldn't see more than a few feet ahead of her.

"Well," Mei said, a note of doubt in her voice. "This looks like the, ah, tunnel."

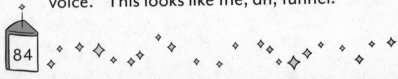

"Did anybody bring a flashlight?" Elvis asked.

The other B-Buds shook their heads.

"I hate to state the obvious," he continued. "But it's really dark in there. I mean, *really* dark. How will we know where we're going?"

"That's a good point," Mei admitted. "I know it's a cave, but I thought Candle Cave wouldn't be so dark inside!"

"We came all this way, though," Amirah said. "We should at least go inside. Maybe there's a light source somewhere and we just haven't spotted it yet."

When no one replied, Amirah knew that her B-Buds needed a little extra encouragement. "Come on, B-Buds! It's our birthday and this has the potential to be the greatest birthday adventure in the history of the world!"

"Or the greatest birthday misadventure," Elvis cracked.

Amirah could tell Elvis was a little scared,

which she definitely understood, yet she felt deep down that they had absolutely nothing to be worried about. She just had to convince him of that without making him feel bad about being scared.

She marched over to Elvis and Mei and linked arms with them. "Safety first," she smiled. "We'll just go in a little ways. And we'll stick together at all times."

Mei nodded. "Okay," she said. "I'm in!"

Elvis took a deep breath. "Let's do this!"

With their heads held high, the B-Buds bravely marched into the dark, shadowy cave. Their footsteps echoed in the darkness.

"Okay it's really dark in here." Inside the cave, Elvis's voice echoed. "Maybe we should go back now."

"Just a little farther." Amirah pushed on. "If only we could see—"

Whooosh!

A sudden sizzling sound zipped through the air, followed by the smell of smoke. Amirah grabbed Elvis's and Mei's arms tighter. If there was a fire somewhere in this cave, they'd have to get out—fast!

But an instant later, two soft flickering lights appeared. Amirah was so relieved that she laughed out loud. "Torches!" she exclaimed.

Sure enough, two torches on the cave wall gleamed with warm light.

"Those aren't torches," Elvis said, pointing. "They're overgrown birthday candles!"

"I think you're right," Amirah replied. "That's why this is called Candle Cave! Those are definitely jumbo birthday candles! Look at the colorful swirls on their sides."

"Look at *everything!*" Mei cried. "Have you ever seen anything like it? Ever, in your whole life?"

Amirah took a moment to look around the cave in astonishment. Overhead, the ceiling was made of rainbow glitter; it sparkled and glowed from the light of the torches. The ground below their feet was covered in confetti. A trickling stream caught Amirah's eye and she walked over to check it out. Next to the stream she saw what appeared to be oversized bubble wands.

"I wonder what happens when I dip one of these in the stream," Amirah murmured. She decided to find out. She dipped the wand in the stream, waved it, and laughed in delight as a group of bubble bats skittered overhead.

"Are those bats?" Mei cried.

"It's okay!" Amirah said quickly. "They're bubble bats!"

Elvis ran over and grabbed a wand and dipped it in the stream to create more bubble bats.

"This is so cool!" he cried.

"As cool as this is, what if these turn into real bats?" Mei wondered, biting her lip.

Amirah didn't think that would happen, but she could tell Mei was nervous. "We should probably keep moving anyway," she said, smil-

ing at her B-Bud and putting the wands back where they had found them.

"Let's see if we can get one of those torches down," Elvis suggested a moment later. "We can carry it through to the other side of the tunnel."

Elvis reached up and tried to pry one of the candle-torches off the cave wall, but all he got for his trouble was a handful of melted wax.

"Well, that was a failure," Elvis said as he peeled the colorful wax off his palms.

With a flicker and a fizzle, the candle-torches unexpectedly burned out.

"Uh-oh," Mei said as the B-Buds were plunged into darkness once more.

"They may be bigger than regular birthday candles, but they still burn out pretty quickly," Elvis said nervously.

"Let's keep going," Amirah encouraged them.

"Are you sure?" Mei exclaimed. "It's just

as dark as it was before—except now we know there are bats and who knows what else!"

"*Bubble bats*," Amirah gently reminded her. "Look, I know it's dark and we can't exactly see anything, but when we needed light before, it just sort of . . . appeared. Let's see if it happens again."

"Okay," Mei said. "But we shouldn't go too much farther without any light. We don't want to get lost in here and never find our way out."

"I know," Amirah said quietly.

The B-Buds took slow, careful steps in the darkness. Finally, Elvis said, "Amirah . . . did you hear that rustling noise?"

"The floor was covered in confetti, remember?" Amirah replied. "Just a little farther. It's just like your bedroom at night. It can be a little spooky when you can't see, but it's still just your room, with all your stuff, and nothing scary. Just like that!"

"Just like that," Elvis repeated. "Of course, there's a night-light in my bedroom," he joked.

"A green gummy bear. But it's not like I use it all the time . . ."

Amirah laughed. She was glad Elvis was being so brave even though he was scared. "I have a night-light too. A rainbow one!"

"Me three," Mei added. "But mine's a purple butterfly."

The group walked a few more careful steps as they talked. Amirah could feel the tension in her B-Buds' arms. She hoped they wouldn't give up. The thought that they'd come so far, only to turn around and have to start over, made her even more determined to find a way through the pitch-black tunnel.

Then, without warning—*whoosh!*

"New birthday candle-torches!" Amirah exclaimed. "Look—you can see the old ones that burned out back there."

"So, maybe if we keep going, even through the darkness, new candle-torches will keep lighting up," Elvis said.

"Maybe *we're* the ones who make them light up," Amirah said. "Maybe they can, I don't know, *sense* us approaching or something . . ."

"In that case, we'd better move fast," Mei said, pointing at the birthday candle-torches. "These ones are burning out as fast at the others did."

"Come on, B-Buds—run!" Amirah yelled.

The B-Buds forgot to be quiet as they raced down the path, reaching the next set of candle-torches right before the previous set extinguished. Amirah wished they could've gone more slowly; the mysterious cave seemed full of wonders that she longed to explore. But when she reminded herself of the girl, and how sad she looked, and how nervous the cave was making her friends, Amirah knew they had to hurry on. *Don't get distracted,* she reminded herself. *We've got to keep going!*

At last, there was a glimmer of light in the distance that was stronger and brighter than

the flames of the candle-torches. The B-Buds recognized it at once.

"Sunlight!" Amirah exclaimed.

"We're almost at the end of the tunnel!" Mei added.

They paused to do a quick victory dance, then kept running.

"I can't believe we made it!" Elvis announced as they finally reached the other side.

"Hey—hang on a minute," Amirah said. "What's that?"

The B-Buds had been so focused on getting through the tunnel before they lost the light that they hadn't realized the trickling stream had widened along the way. At the other end of the tunnel, it had pooled into a small underground lake with an island in the middle.

On the island sat three beautifully wrapped presents.

"Do you think those are . . . for us?" Elvis asked.

"Three presents, three of us," Amirah said. "And it *is* our birthday . . ."

"What if it's a trap?" Mei asked.

Amirah shook her head. "Not in the Magical Land of Birthdays."

"We already have the map, though. Shouldn't we just keep going?" Mei asked. "Besides, who wants to wade through all that yucky mud?"

For Amirah, though, the lure of the presents was too strong.

"I don't mind mud," Amirah said. "Besides, I have a feeling it's probably more like chocolate pudding."

She took off her shoes and placed them by the side of the pond. It wasn't deep at all, just barely past her ankles. "Here goes," she said.

Squish. Squelch. Squish.

Amirah might have thought that Mei was right about the mud being yucky—except every step she took released the heady scent of chocolate. "This mud smells just like the filling for chocolate mud cake!" Amirah said.

"My friend Holden had chocolate mud cake at his birthday party last year!" Elvis exclaimed. "It was so good!"

Suddenly Amirah shrieked. "Eww! Something's tickling my toes!"

"Is it a snake?" Mei exclaimed.

Amirah pulled her foot out of the pond and peeled something colorful off it. "No," she replied. "Just a gummy worm."

When Amirah reached the island, she knew it had been worth it. The three presents were topped with glittery gift tags—and the tags had their names. There was one for her, wrapped in pink sparkly paper; one for Mei, wrapped in purple polka-dot paper; and one for Elvis, wrapped in green-striped paper.

"Happy birthday, B-Buds!" Amirah exclaimed as she gave her friends their gifts.

Elvis opened his first. It was a shiny metal

tube that could be extended several feet or collapsed on itself until it was pocket size. "Pretty cool," he said. "I'm not sure what to do with it, though."

"I have no idea what to do with my present either," Mei said as she held up a pair of glasses. Instead of smooth glass, though, the lenses were faceted like a gemstone. She put them on and made a funny face. "How do I look? I feel like a fly."

"They look great! But too bad those glasses give you a fly's eyes instead of a fly's wings," Amirah replied.

"I could always wear them like a headband," Mei said, laughing as she pushed the glasses on top of her head.

"Pretty! Like a tiara!" Amirah said.

"Open your present, Amirah," Elvis encouraged.

When Amirah opened her gift, she understood why the B-Buds seemed a little disappointed. "Huh. A tin whistle," she said. Then she held it out to Elvis. "There must be a mistake. This one's probably for you. After all, you're the musician."

Elvis shook his head. "I don't think the Magical Land of Birthdays makes mistakes," he said. "That gift definitely said 'Amirah' on it. I'll play you a song, though."

When Elvis tried to play the whistle, though, it didn't make a sound. "Too bad," he said as he handed it back to Amirah. "It's broken."

"Well, just because we can't hear it doesn't mean it's broken," Amirah pointed out.

Mei looked alarmed. "Are you talking about the bats?" she asked. "Bats can hear at different frequencies than humans! It was one thing when they were flying away from us, but do we really want them flying *toward* us?"

"Uh . . . that wasn't exactly what I had in mind," Amirah replied. "But now that you mention it—let's get out of here!"

The B-Buds raced out the tunnel, laughing and shrieking. In the bright sunshine, they paused so Amirah could wipe off her feet and put her shoes back on. Then they set off down the other side of the mountain. The B-Buds soon discovered that it was even easier to climb *down* the mountain than *up*. As they made their way down the trail, the rock candy smoothed back into candy buttons. Eventually even the candy buttons receded until the friends found themselves walking on a smooth surface.

"The ground has changed," Mei commented.

Amirah leaned over and used her finger to draw a heart on the path. Then, to everyone's astonishment, she popped her finger in her mouth!

Amirah laughed at the B-Buds' shocked expressions. "Don't worry," she told them. "It's just cake frosting! The glossy kind that you can pipe designs on."

"Of course it is," Elvis said as he started to

laugh too. Then he tilted his head to the side. "Do you hear that, B-Buds?" he asked.

"More music?" Mei guessed.

"No . . . not this time," Elvis replied, still listening intently. "It sounds like a . . . rushing noise."

"Rushing?" Amirah asked. "Would a unicorn rush? I guess if she did, it would be more like a gallop. They have hooves, after all."

"Like horses," Mei chimed in.

"I'm pretty sure it's not a unicorn," Elvis said. "Or anything alive. I just can't . . ."

Amirah shivered as a cool breeze blew past them. Were they so close to the Rainbow Forest that they could feel cooler air circulating around the shade-giving trees?

When the friends rounded a curve in the path, they solved both mysteries. They found themselves standing on the bank of a rushing river, with whipped-cream whitecaps swirling over the deep waters.

"There's the rushing sound," Elvis said.

"And that's where the cool breeze came from," Amirah added.

Mei scrunched up her face. "Oh no," she said. "I don't remember seeing the river on the other side of the mountains. I remember seeing something about a stream, but not a giant river. I'm sorry, B-Buds. How are we going to cross it?"

"It's not your fault!" Amirah assured her. "This land is new to all of us! Besides, there has to be a bridge somewhere, right?" Amirah asked.

"Or maybe a boat?" Elvis suggested.

"Look at those rapids," Mei said. "I don't know how to pilot a boat through such rough water. Do you?"

"No . . . I guess not," Elvis admitted. "But we're in the Magical Land of Birthdays! So the boat has got to be magical too!"

"But there *is* no boat," Mei reminded him.

"Oh. Right," Elvis said. "Well, let's check the

map. There has to be a way to cross the river. I mean, surely somebody before us has figured out a way to get across."

Amirah took a few steps away from the riverbank and turned around so that the spray wouldn't get on the map. "This explains it, Mei!" she cried a moment later. "The river is called the Silly Stream River! That's why you thought it was a stream! That's a really easy mistake to make!"

Mei smiled gratefully at Amirah.

Amirah studied the map. The Silly Stream River wound its way across the entire land, swirling and swooping as it cut a path through the fields and the forest. If there were any bridges— or even any docks with boats—the map didn't indicate them.

What if there really isn't a way across? Amirah wondered. She didn't want to say those words aloud. She didn't even want to think them. The

Magical Land of Birthdays was no place to lose hope . . . or admit defeat.

The river on the map sparkled like sapphires and diamonds, as if actual sunlight was glinting on real water. Amirah kept studying it, trying to find a way across. But the map didn't offer any solutions to their problem.

Finally, Amirah stood up and looked around for her B-Buds. Elvis and Mei had wandered off a little way and seemed to be checking out an incredible tree. Instead of leaves, the tree was covered in helium balloons of all colors. The balloons swayed back and forth in the breeze, making rainbow shadows on the ground.

Amirah guessed that it was the incredible tree that had first captured her B-Buds' attention. Now, though, Elvis was drumming a cool rhythm on the tree trunk while Mei gracefully twirled on one of the lower branches.

"Hey, B-Buds," Amirah called. "I've searched and searched the map, but I can't find a clear way across the river. But I do have some ideas."

"Hit it," Elvis said, still drumming.

"We can change course a little," Amirah began. "Instead of sticking to the path, we'll walk along the riverbank. I figure there's a pretty good chance of one of two things happening. First, we'll either stumble on a way to cross the river—a bridge or maybe even a boat. Something that's not marked on the map."

"What's your other idea?" Mei asked. She leaped up to grab the branch above her and climbed up.

"Well . . . maybe the river isn't so deep and fast everywhere," Amirah said. "Just because it's rushing rapids *here* doesn't mean it isn't a calm little stream elsewhere. Know what I mean?"

"Yeah," Mei said. "But, we still don't know if either one of those will happen."

"That's true," Amirah said. "I could be wrong on both counts. If only there was a way to see . . ."

When Amirah's voice trailed off unexpectedly, Elvis stopped drumming midbeat.

"What is it?" he asked. "Is something wrong?"

"No, I just had another idea," Amirah said. "Mei, how high can you climb?"

"Not as high as I want to," Mei replied. "There's too many balloons! I can't see which branch to grab next."

"Hmm," Amirah said, frowning. "I was thinking that maybe if you could climb all the way to the top of the tree, you could *see* how the river flows. And you could tell us if there's an area that doesn't look so rough, or even better, if there's a bridge—"

Mei gasped.

"You okay?" Amirah asked.

"My birthday glasses!" Mei exclaimed. "I forgot I was wearing them on my head—then I looked down to see you and they slipped off

my head, over my eyes—and now I can see the branches perfectly!"

"What? How?" Elvis asked.

"I think it's birthday magic," Mei said. "Instead of the whole balloon, I only see the outlines. It's amazing!"

Mei started to climb the tree, higher and higher, until she disappeared behind the thick canopy of colorful balloons. Amirah and Elvis stood at the base of the tree, trying to catch a glimpse of Mei.

"There must be thousands of balloons up here." Mei's voice floated down to them.

"What else can you see?" Amirah called back.

"Still balloon outlines," Mei replied. "Bunches and bunches of balloons."

Amirah and Elvis exchanged a worried glance. Amirah hadn't expected the balloon tree to be so big that it got in their way.

"Don't worry—I have a plan," Mei said. "Once I get a little higher, I'll push some of these balloons out of the way and then, hopefully, I'll have a pretty clear view of—oh! Oh! Oh no!"

"Mei!" Amirah shrieked. "What happened? Are you okay?"

There was no response.

CHAPTER EIGHT

"**MEI!**" Amirah and Elvis yelled at the same time.

"Something happened," Amirah said. "Something's wrong."

"Maybe not," Elvis said. He pointed at the ground under the tree. "She didn't fall."

"Mei! Can you hear us?" Amirah yelled at the top of her voice.

"I'm okay," Mei said. She sounded even farther away. "I'm—"

"What happened? Can you see anything?" Elvis yelled.

Amirah and Elvis stared up at the sky, completely speechless. A purple balloon had broken free from the balloon tree and was floating into the sky . . .

And it was carrying Mei with it!

"B-Buds!" Mei cried. Her voice was faint and far away, but if Amirah strained, she could still hear her. "I found a way across the river!"

"Of course!" Elvis exclaimed, smacking his

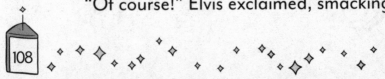

forehead. "We thought of traveling by land, by sea—"

"But we never thought of traveling by air!" Amirah finished for him.

"Quick! Grab a balloon and come with me!" Mei said.

She was floating farther and farther away. Amirah knew there wasn't a moment to lose. She and Elvis jumped up as high as they could. Amirah grabbed a golden string and yanked— hard!

The string snapped off the branch. With her heart pounding, Amirah squeezed her hand even tighter around the balloon's string. She felt a gentle tug at her wrist as the string pulled taut. She looked up and saw that the balloon was pink.

Then, suddenly, the balloon lifted her into the air!

Amirah's nerves soon gave way to a dizzy- ing exhilaration. Traveling by floating balloon

109

was more fun than she ever could've imagined. High in the clear blue sky, she could see Mei bobbing along in front of her. Elvis, dangling from a green balloon, wasn't far behind.

"Look! Look at the river!" Mei called as they floated over it.

Amirah glanced down at the roaring river and saw that the water was even clearer than she had expected. She could see the bottom of the riverbed, which glittered with more rock candy. There was even a school of gummy fish darting back and forth, their fins glinting in the sunlight that sliced through the water.

"Incredible," Amirah breathed.

"Hey, B-Buds?" Elvis called. "I have a question. How are we going to get down—whoaaaaaaaaaa!"

Without warning, Elvis's balloon suddenly plunged several feet. Amirah and Mei screamed.

"I'm okay! I'm okay!" Elvis said, breathing

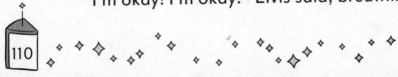

hard. "Wow. That was, uh, that was a surprise. I don't know what's up with—ahhhhhhhhhhh!"

Just as unexpectedly, Elvis's balloon suddenly rocketed several feet into the air. Amirah and Mei screamed again.

Elvis, looking a little pale, opened his mouth—but this time, no words came out.

With her free hand, Amirah rummaged in her pocket for her sprinkles and shook a few into her mouth to help herself calm down. *Calm down,* she thought suddenly. *Calm* down! *Of course! That's it!*

"Elvis!" Amirah yelled. "You're a genius!"

"I'm a what?" he asked, confused.

"You figured out how to control the balloons!" Amirah continued. "Just say *up* and—wheeeee!"

Since Amirah was expecting it, she didn't panic when her balloon suddenly soared upward. "And then you can always go dowwwwwwwnnnnnnnnn!" she said, giggling as her balloon swooped toward the ground. It felt like riding on a flying roller coaster!

Soon all the B-Buds were laughing as they made their balloons go up and down through the sky. At last, though, Amirah knew it was time to continue their journey on land instead of by air.

"Down," she told her balloon. "Down, down, down."

The balloon lowered her to the ground until her toes grazed the sandy graham cracker–crumb riverbank. "Thank you," Amirah told her balloon as she let go of the string. Then she watched as the balloon floated back to the balloon tree. Soon it disappeared among the hundreds of other colorful balloons that were swaying in the breeze.

On the other side of the river, the air was even cooler. It almost felt heavier. Amirah moved closer to Mei and Elvis, and all three of them looked toward the shadowy forest.

"What do you think?" Mei finally asked. "Should we . . . check it out?"

"Let's do it," Amirah replied, nodding her head. "After all, we've come all this way . . ."

The B-Buds were quiet as they slipped into the forest. The trees here were the most magnificent trees Amirah had ever seen. Where regular trees might have moss hanging from their branches, the trees in the Rainbow Forest had loops of shimmery rainbow-colored ribbons. The ribbons were curled just like the ones used to decorate birthday presents.

"I think this is definitely the Rainbow Forest," Amirah whispered as she and her friends looked up at the amazing rainbow canopy above their heads. The ribbons brushed against Amirah's skin, making her shiver a little as the friends moved deeper into the woods. Up ahead, she thought she could see a faint light glimmering in a clearing. *Could that be Cara the Unicorn?* Amirah wondered. She imagined that a unicorn's horn would cast a beautiful light.

As Amirah moved faster, Mei and Elvis did too. When they reached the clearing, though, there was no sign of a unicorn.

Instead, the friends realized that they had stumbled upon a party. Well, not a party, exactly. There were no guests anywhere to be seen. Just a long table, decorated with a sea-green table-cloth and blue-and-pink plates. There were shells scattered along the table and tiny sand-castles beside each plate; tall glasses of pink lemonade with cherries bobbing on top; and a beautiful, three-tiered cake decorated with shimmery scales, sugar pearls, and candy stars.

"This is someone's party," Amirah observed. "It's a—it's a mermaid party."

"Look at the ground," Mei said, pointing down. "How did all this sand get into the middle of the woods?"

Elvis licked his lips. "I'm really thirsty," he

said. "Do you think they'd mind if I drank some lemonade?"

Amirah glanced around. "I don't know," she said. "There's no one here to ask. But . . ."

Elvis walked toward the table and reached for one of the glasses. Just as he was about to pick it up, it dissolved into nothingness.

"Wait a minute! None of this is real," he said, trying to lift one of the seashells. It, too, vanished into a silvery mist.

"This isn't a party," Amirah suddenly realized. "It's like . . . the *memory* of a party. Or an *idea*. Something that doesn't actually exist in the real world."

"Is it just me, or are all the colors fading?" Mei asked, frowning. "They're, like, washed out."

"It's not just you," Elvis agreed. "It kind of looks like this whole party is going to . . . disappear."

"Like the girl!" Amirah exclaimed.

"Remember how she was here but not here? And she seemed to . . . flicker? And fade away?"

"Do you think she's connected to this lonely party?" Elvis asked.

Amirah nodded. She closed her eyes for a moment and listened to what her heart was telling her. "I do," she said. "I can't really explain it—I mean, I don't have any proof—but I really believe they're connected somehow. And I'm almost positive she's one of our B-Buds."

"But everything else in the Magical Land of Birthdays is so bright and colorful," Mei pointed out. "Why would this gloomy party be connected to us or one of our B-Buds?"

"I'm not sure," Amirah replied. What Mei said was perfectly rational. But in her heart, Amirah felt certain that the party was somehow connected to the girl, who she was sure was one of their B-Buds. And she needed their help.

"There's a light," Elvis suddenly said.

The girls looked where he was pointing.

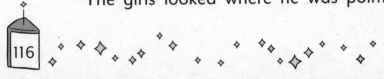

Sure enough, on the other side of the clearing, a silver light glimmered. It hovered in the branches of the trees, just above their heads.

In silence, the B-Buds moved toward the light. Amirah reached out to push aside the tangled ribbons. Then she gasped in amazement.

"B-Buds! We did it!" she cried. "We found Cara the Unicorn!"

CHAPTER NINE

"CARA THE UNICORN IS . . . a piñata?" Elvis asked doubtfully, staring into the trees.

"I thought Cara was going to be a real unicorn," Mei added.

Disappointment flickered through Amirah. She didn't want to admit it, but she'd expected Cara the Unicorn to be real too. But there was no doubt that the unicorn before them was a piñata. A stunning piñata—gorgeous, even—made of silvery tissue paper, with a rainbow mane of ribbon roses and a silver horn that seemed lit from within. *That's where the light is coming from,* Amirah thought.

The piñata hung from a silver ribbon that was tied to a branch. As it spun and twisted in the gentle breeze, Amirah knew that there was nothing real, or lifelike, about it.

But nothing here is what it seems, Amirah reminded herself. If she'd learned anything during her adventures in the Magical Land of Birthdays,

it was that anything was possible, anything in the whole world. Especially on a birthday.

"She's so beautiful," Amirah whispered, reaching up to rest her hand on the piñata's side. For the briefest instant, she thought she felt something. A quiver, maybe, or a pulse. But she knew it was just her imagination. Cara the Unicorn was just a piñata, after all.

"Stand back, B-Bud," Elvis said, his voice interrupting Amirah's thoughts. She turned around and saw that he was carrying his present. Fully extended, the silver tube was three feet long. It almost looked like a tree branch.

"What's that for?" Amirah asked.

"That's a piñata," Elvis replied, pointing the silver stick at Cara. "And piñatas are full of treats and surprises and good stuff. So I'm guessing we need to break it open."

"Ooh, remember the rock?" Mei asked excitedly. "When it cracked open, we found a map inside!"

"And the map helped us find our way to the unicorn," Elvis added. "I bet our next clue is inside the piñata!"

A slight frown flickered across Amirah's face. Everything her friends said made sense. But breaking open this piñata felt wrong somehow, in ways she couldn't quite explain. The piñata shimmered as it swayed gently in the breeze. Amirah already knew she couldn't bear to watch something so beautiful be destroyed.

As Amirah thought about what to do next, her hand still resting on the piñata's side, a silvery mist swirled around their ankles.

"Where's this misty stuff coming from?" Mei wondered, trying to wave it away. It continued to fill the clearing, snaking around their legs, their knees, their waists . . .

"That party, I bet," Elvis replied. He raised the silver stick above his head. "Let's break open the piñata while we can still see it."

Suddenly, Amirah felt it again—a tremble deep within the piñata.

"Wait," Amirah said. She was more convinced than ever that this was no ordinary piñata. But how could she convince her friends? She had no proof.

Amirah held out her hand. "Can I have the tube?" she asked.

"Sure," Elvis said with a shrug. "Give it a good whack! It should be easy without a blindfold. I can't wait to find out what's inside!"

As Elvis placed the stick in her hand, Amirah was surprised to find that it felt strangely warm for a piece of metal. Then she felt something else—the faintest pulse, the slightest quiver.

Just like when she had touched the piñata.

Amirah lifted the stick high into the air. Instead of hitting the piñata, though, she gently touched the stick to the silver string from which it hung.

Zzzzzzzzzzzzzzzzzzzzzzzzz!

The sound of sparks crackling filled the clearing, but Amirah barely noticed. She was too busy shielding her eyes from the startling light, so warm, so bright, so beautiful that it was almost blinding.

Almost.

Amirah couldn't help but watch through her fingers. The shimmering light was devouring the string like a sparkling candle on a birthday cake. Not just the string, though. It crackled over the unicorn piñata, until the whole thing blazed with such brightness that Amirah really did have to look away.

Within seconds, the warmth faded away, and it grew quiet enough in the clearing that Amirah could hear a soft *thud.* Then another, and another, and another.

It almost sounded like hoofbeats.

She opened her eyes.

Across the clearing stood Cara the Unicorn.

CHAPTER TEN

NOT A PIÑATA, not a stuffed animal, but real in every way, from her flowing mane to her eyes, which were as dark and shimmery as a lake reflecting a full moon at midnight. All the parts of Cara that had once been silver were now gold, beaming with a warmth and brightness that filled Amirah's heart with happiness.

Cara bobbed her head, making her mane cascade like a rainbow-tinged waterfall, and pawed at the ground with her shimmery hooves. She was so lovely, so magical, so majestic that Amirah almost wanted to bow to her.

Instead, Amirah nodded her head at Cara.

Then, to her astonishment, Cara nodded back!

"I'm Amirah," Amirah said, even though she had a funny feeling that Cara already knew that. She held out her hand, palm up, and waited, barely daring to breathe.

Cara took a few steps toward Amirah and gently nuzzled her hand. Just standing near the

unicorn made Amirah feel a little dizzy. Meeting a real unicorn had always seemed like a day-dream, a fantasy that could only occur in her imagination. But in the Magical Land of Birth-days, anything could happen.

Amirah closed her eyes from pure joy and imagined how incredible it would be to explore this wild, wonderful world with Cara by her side. Cara, she knew, could show her everything. Cara could help her find her way. They'd roam the rocky roads, skip through the field of cake ball flowers, climb the craggy mountains, and finally, explore Sparkle City at the tippy-top of the island—

"Amirah!"

The urgency in Mei's voice pierced Amirah's daydream. In all the excitement, she'd almost forgotten about her B-Buds.

"The mist," Mei continued. "It's getting thicker. How are we going to get out of the forest?"

Amirah had been so captivated by Cara the Unicorn's appearance that she had failed to notice the rising mist. It was thicker than before, thick enough to cut through with a swipe of her hand. Yet there seemed to be no way to clear it. No matter how much Amirah, Mei, and Elvis tried to wave the mist away, it grew thicker and thicker. Soon, Amirah knew, the B-Buds wouldn't even be able to see across the clearing.

They wouldn't even be able to see each other.

Suddenly, Amirah gasped.

"What's wrong?" Elvis asked. She could hear him, but could barely make out his silhouette among the swirling mist.

"My dream," Amirah cried. "It ended in clouds of mist—just like this!"

"Is that happening again?" Mei said urgently. "Is our adventure almost over?"

"It can't end like this," Amirah exclaimed.

"It just can't. We haven't found the girl—we haven't figured out how to help her—"

Amirah spun around. She could still see Cara, glimmering at the edge of the clearing. The unicorn seemed to emit a sense of calm; if she was concerned about the rising mist, she didn't show it.

"If this is just a dream—if we all wake up at our homes—how will we find each other again?" Elvis asked.

"No," Amirah said, shaking her head. "It doesn't end yet. Not now. Not like this. I won't let it."

Amirah's emotions swirled almost as wildly as the mist. Her hands were trembling a little as she unscrewed the cap on her container of sprinkles and popped a few in her mouth.

Think, she ordered herself. *Think, think, think. Everyone is counting on you.*

It wouldn't help to panic or freak out. Besides, that wasn't Amirah's style. She snacked on a few more sprinkles as she racked her brain. What had they learned so far in the Magical Land of Birthdays? What had this special place been trying to tell them?

Find Cara the Unicorn

The message in the sprinkles—and the map in the rock—hadn't led Amirah and the B-Buds to the mysterious girl. They'd sent them on a search for this enchanting creature. Then, almost by accident, the B-Buds had freed Cara from her piñata form.

Why, though?

Why?

Suddenly an idea sparked in Amirah's mind. "Cara!" she cried. Even the unicorn was hard to see now through the mist. "Where is she? Where is the mysterious girl?"

The mist swirled. The silence stretched.

Then Cara the Unicorn dipped her head and pointed her horn across the clearing.

A sparkling rainbow sprang from her horn,

evaporating the mist and illuminating the forest.

Not just the forest.

Amirah blinked in disbelief. There, standing in the beam of light, was the mysterious girl she'd spotted by the candy-apple tree. The very same one from her dream.

How long has she been there? Amirah wondered.

Remembering how the girl had run away from them before, Amirah knew that she had to act fast. She rushed across the clearing, with Mei and Elvis right behind her.

"Please don't go!" Amirah cried. "We've been looking for you everywhere. Everywhere!"

The girl blinked in surprise. "Me?" she asked. "You've been looking for *me?*" Her voice was soft, with an accent that Amirah recognized as Australian.

"Yes! Since we saw you back at the strawberry field," Amirah said. "Didn't you see us?"

There was a long pause.

"Yes," the girl finally said, her voice barely more than a whisper. She stared at the ground. "But I didn't want to ruin your day."

The B-Buds exchanged a troubled glance.

"Ruin our day?" Amirah asked. "What do you mean?"

"Yeah, how could you ruin our day?" Elvis asked, perplexed.

The girl held out her hand near one of the trees. Astonishingly, the chocolate-brown trunk faded to pale tan; the bright green leaves grew withered and gray. "Everywhere I go, the color fades away," she said. "It's like the whole world gets as sad as I am. And when I saw the three of you . . ."

As her voice trailed off, Cara stepped forward and nuzzled her arm. The act of kindness seemed to encourage the girl.

"You seemed so happy. Like you were having so much fun together," the girl said sadly. "And I just . . . I didn't want to ruin it."

Amirah's heart swelled with sympathy. They'd been so worried about this girl—whoever she was—and at the same time she'd been worrying about *them.*

"We were just talking about our birthdays," Elvis spoke up. "See, this is so crazy, but we all have the same birthday—today . . ."

His voice trailed off as the girl's eyes widened. "But today is *my* birthday," she said.

"Really?" Mei exclaimed. "That means you're one of us—one of the B-Buds! You were right, Amirah!"

"That stands for Birthday Buds," Elvis added. He stuck out his hand. "Nice to meet you, B-Bud! I'm Elvis!"

"I'm Mei."

"And I'm Amirah," Amirah offered.

A small, soft smile flickered across the girl's face. "I'm Olivia," she replied.

Amirah impulsively gave her a hug. "Happy birthday, Olivia," she said.

Olivia hugged her back, but her smile wavered.

"Since we're officially B-Buds now, do you want to tell us what's wrong?" Amirah asked.

Olivia looked away. "I don't want to trouble you on your birthdays," she said shyly.

"Are you kidding?" Amirah asked. "That's what B-Buds are for!"

"Yeah!" Mei chimed in. "We want to help! However we can!"

Olivia tried to smile at her new friends. "It's just—today's my birthday," she began. "I mean, you already know that. I've been planning my birthday party for months. A mermaid party on the beach—"

"The beach?" Elvis asked in surprise. "In January?"

Olivia nodded. "In Australia, where I live, it's summertime," she explained.

"No way!" Elvis exclaimed.

"Of course," Mei said. "The seasons are opposite in the southern hemisphere."

"Tell us all about your party plans," Amirah encouraged. "I love hearing about birthdays almost as much as I love celebrating them!"

"We were going to put a big table on the beach and cover it with seashells and glitter," Olivia said sadly. "And make seashell tiaras and sea wands . . . We were going to have a sandcastle-building contest and a seashell scavenger hunt. Then, when the sun set, we were going to hang up all these jellyfish lanterns my mum and I made, and my dad was going to build a bonfire of driftwood. And I painted a treasure chest and put all the party favors in it—soap shaped like seahorses and sandcastle snow globes and chocolate starfish."

"It sounds amazing!" Amirah cried, totally captivated.

"Thanks," Olivia mumbled. "I think it

would've been. But now it's going to rain, and not just a little drizzly rain, but buckets and buckets of rain! There's no way we can have my party on the beach. Not with the kind of storm that's brewing."

The B-Buds sat in silence for a moment.

"Well . . . can you move your party inside?" Elvis finally asked.

Olivia shrugged. "That's what my mum said. But our living room isn't nearly as right for a mermaid party at the beach," she said. "No sand-castle contest, no seashell scavenger hunt, no driftwood bonfire. Just a lot of pretending at being mermaids in a living room, like we're little kids. I don't even have a proper party dress and I'm *not* wearing my bathing suit in the house; that would be ridiculous! It's going to be the most un-magical birthday ever. It almost . . . it almost makes me want to skip it altogether and cancel my party."

Amirah sucked in her breath sharply. "Skip

your birthday and cancel your party?" she exclaimed. "Nuh-uh. No way. Not on our watch. Right, B-Buds?"

"Right!" Mei and Elvis said at the same time.

Then Elvis cleared his throat. "Uh . . . what exactly did you have in mind?" he asked Amirah.

The truth was that Amirah hadn't quite figured that out yet. But she wasn't worried. She snacked on a few sprinkles as she thought it over.

"Olivia," Amirah began. "A birthday is important. A birthday *matters.* It's the most special day of the year because it's the day *you* were born. There was nobody like you in the whole wide world until the day you were born—your birth-day—when that changed *forever!*"

This time, when Olivia smiled, it was less wavery than before.

"The thing about birthdays is that their joy can last you the whole year," Amirah continued. "I call it living the birthday lifestyle."

"Like—every day is your birthday?" Elvis asked in confusion.

"Not exactly," Amirah said. "Your birthday is one and only! But the way I feel on my birthday—special and loved and happy—well, I want to feel like that every day. That's another reason why I always carry sprinkles in my pocket. Here—hold out your hands!"

The B-Buds stuck out their hands so Amirah could shake some sprinkles into their palms. Then everyone munched on the sprinkles together.

"See what I mean? Sprinkles make every-thing feel a little bit like a party!" Amirah said. Then she turned back to Olivia. "I don't know if your birthday party would feel un-magical at your house. I mean, I think all birthdays are magic . . . even when they're not perfect.

"But here's what I do know," she continued. "We're in the most magical place in the universe. I mean, it's right in the name—the Magical Land of Birthdays! So this is my idea . . . let's celebrate *here!*"

"Here?" Olivia repeated.

"Right here," Amirah said, holding her arms open wide. "There's a table set up for a party right over in the clearing. It's not, you know, the beach, but I know we can make the best of—"

"Oh!" Mei suddenly exclaimed, interrupting Amirah. She pulled out the map and unrolled it. "Sorry I cut you off! But I thought I remembered seeing a beach on the map. Look, there's one right here. It's called Celebration Shore!"

"Genius!" Amirah's eyes lit up. "We can have your beachy birthday party there!" she told Olivia. "I'm certain that birthdays *never* get rained out in the Magical Land of Birthdays."

"One question, though," Elvis said. "How are we going to get to Celebration Shore? It's really far away according to the map."

"That's a good point," Mei said thoughtfully

as she traced a winding path across the map. "The forest is in the very center of the island, which means a long journey to the beach, which is way off to the east side of the island."

Amirah snapped her fingers. "The balloon tree," she suggested.

"That's possible," Mei said. "But . . . dangerous."

"Dangerous? What do you mean?" Olivia asked, her eyes growing wide.

Mei told Olivia about how they'd traveled by balloon across the river. "Here's the thing, though," she said. "That was a pretty short trip— just a few minutes, from one side of the river to the other. To travel by balloon all the way across the Magical Land of Birthdays would take a lot longer. What if one of the balloons popped and dropped us somewhere *without* a balloon tree? Then we'd have to walk anyway . . . and I don't think we'd make it before dark."

"Does it even get dark in the Magical Land of Birthdays?" Amirah wondered. But no one knew for sure.

"Here's another thing that could go wrong. What if the wind blew us in the wrong direction?" Elvis added. "Those balloons were not exactly easy to pilot."

"True," Amirah said. She was still determined to think of another way to get to the beach.

Then Amirah remembered the whistle in her pocket. She pulled it out and turned it over and over in her hands.

Just because we can't hear it doesn't mean it's broken, she remembered.

Cara the Unicorn nudged Amirah's shoulder. Amirah absentmindedly reached up to stroke Cara's mane.

The unicorn nudged her again, more insistently this time. When she nudged Amirah even harder, Amirah almost dropped the whistle.

"Whoa!" Amirah cried. "Okay, I get it. You're trying to tell me something. Is it about . . . the whistle?"

Cara nodded enthusiastically.

Amirah took a deep breath and put the whistle to her lips. She didn't know any songs, but she moved her fingers along the small holes as she blew into it. The sweetest melody filled the air. It was like a cross between wind chimes and bird trills and was so beautiful that even after the last note faded, no one spoke.

CHAPTER ELEVEN

FOR A FEW MOMENTS, nothing happened.

Then . . .

Amirah felt it before she heard or saw what was happening. The ground trembled underfoot again, just like it had when the sprinkles had spelled out a secret message for her. Amirah knelt down to see if there was another message to decode.

Before she spotted any sprinkles, though, she heard the unmistakable sound of hoofbeats galloping toward them.

More unicorns? Amirah wondered in astonishment as she scrambled to her feet.

No. Not this time. Cara was the only unicorn in the Magical Land of Birthdays.

But the B-Buds would soon realize that Cara had three very special friends.

"Carousel horses!" Olivia shrieked with glee.

Cara's friends were the most beautiful

horses that Amirah had ever seen. White and silver, dappled gray, glossy black. Their manes were entwined with velvet ribbons and real roses; their bridles gleamed with tiny bells that chimed whenever they moved. Amirah could have gazed upon them for hours.

Then, as if on cue, the horses knelt before the B-Buds. It was an invitation to mount them and set off for a ride!

Olivia laughed as a dappled horse adorned with blue roses licked her hand. Amirah and Mei looked at each other and smiled. Olivia's mood was already brightening—just like the Magical Land of Birthdays, now that the mist was evaporating.

Then a look of concern passed over Mei's face. "Hold on," she said, her forehead wrinkled with worry. "There are four of us . . . and only three of them."

Could one carousel horse carry two B-Buds? Maybe. But it seemed like too great a favor to ask. Amirah set her thoughts to spinning once more, trying to think of a new plan, any plan, when something astonishing happened.

Cara the Unicorn, that most enchanting and magical creature, nuzzled Amirah's face . . . and knelt before her!

"Problem solved," Elvis declared. "Come on, B-Buds! It's time to saddle up!"

Once the friends had climbed aboard, the magical creatures stood up and began to gallop through the forest, cleverly dodging trees and leaping over stones. Riding a unicorn—a real unicorn—was an honor Amirah had never expected, and an experience she'd never forget. She wrapped her arms around Cara's neck as Cara galloped out of the clearing, with the carousel horses following her. Her silky mane smelled like birthday cake.

Amirah didn't know how long they rode. Soon the forest gave way to fields, fields turned into meadows, and eventually the landscape changed again. The grass lengthened, transforming into tall stalks of sea grass that swayed back and forth in the brisk ocean breeze. Despite the thundering hooves, she could hear another sound—the ocean waves crashing on the shore. She breathed in deeply, expecting to smell the crisp, salty smell of the beach.

But nothing in the Magical Land of Birthdays was exactly as it seemed. Here, the beach smelled like butter and brown sugar!

Cara and the carousel horses climbed the crest of the dunes, and at last, the B-Buds could see the beach. They had arrived at Celebration Shore. It was the most beautiful coast Amirah had ever seen. The ocean sparkled in the golden sunshine as waves crashed on the shore in a creamy froth. The sand looked so soft and inviting that Amirah couldn't wait to kick off her shoes and dance on the beach.

The B-Buds jumped down from their carousel horses and raced toward the ocean. Amirah paused to stroke Cara's forehead after dismounting. "Thank you," she whispered.

Cara nuzzled Amirah's neck. Amirah knew in that moment that Cara was saying goodbye. She threw her arms around Cara's neck, breathing in the sweet smell of her mane one last time when it hit her . . . This was just goodbye for now. As she inhaled Cara's sweet birthday cake smell, Amirah's head filled with a vision of herself riding Cara again, this time through an unfamiliar landscape that Amirah knew was a part of the Magical Land of Birthdays she had not seen yet. But she would see it someday. She would be back. She was sure of it.

Amirah released Cara, who gave her one last nuzzle. Then the unicorn galloped toward the ocean, with the carousel horses following behind her. The B-Buds watched as Cara and her friends galloped through the surf, sending sparkling drops of water into the air, until they disappeared into the distance.

"Come on, B-Buds!" Elvis hollered. "Let's go!"

Laughing and shrieking with glee, the B-Buds ran around the beach—all except for Olivia. When Amirah realized that Olivia wasn't with them, she doubled back to her newest friend.

"You okay?" Amirah called, worried that perhaps their trip to the beach hadn't helped Olivia feel better about her special day.

But when Olivia looked over at her, Amirah noticed a look of wonder on her face. She also noticed that the colors around Olivia were now as vibrant as they were in the rest of the land. Amirah smiled, knowing this meant her B-Bud was no longer feeling sad.

"Amirah," Olivia whispered. "That treasure chest . . . It looks just like the one I made for my beach birthday party back home . . ."

Amirah turned around to see a turquoise treasure chest nestled in the sand. It had gleaming brass hinges and a curved lid. A shiver of

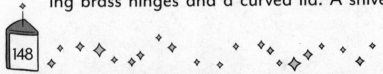

anticipation tingled down Amirah's spine as she wondered what might be inside.

"Come on," she told Olivia. "Let's open it!"

The two B-Buds knelt beside the chest and flipped up the latch. Then, together, they eased open the lid.

Amirah and Olivia both gasped. Somehow, the treasure chest was enormous on the inside, and jam-packed with everything Olivia would need for an *indoor* mermaid birthday party! There were shimmery drapes for the walls that would make her living room look like it was underwater, streamers that looked like seaweed, a pin-the-tail-on-the-mermaid game. There was even a bubble machine that would send tiny bubbles floating through the air! Best of all, there was a shell-pink party dress made of shimmery fabric that was just Olivia's size. Amirah knew that her B-Bud would look gorgeous wearing it.

"This is incredible!" Olivia gasped. "But how will I get all this home for my party?"

Amirah thought about that for a moment. "I don't think you're supposed to bring it home," she said slowly. "I think you use what's in the trunk for your party here, and then as inspiration to make your own party at home!"

"Inspiration?" Olivia repeated. "I'm not sure I follow."

"It's just like decorating a cake," Amirah said. "You have to use your imagination!"

Olivia still looked a little confused, so Amirah continued. "You have bubbles at home, right?" Olivia nodded. "Well, put them out at your party. Everyone can blow bubbles to make your living room look like an underwater kingdom!" Amirah took another look in the trunk. "You can hang green streamers to look like seaweed . . . and use glitter markers to decorate a dress to make it shimmery."

Amirah paused. "Hmm, what could you make the dress out of though?"

"I'm actually pretty good at sewing," Olivia

said shyly. "Maybe I can use the material from a sheet to make a dress and then decorate it to look shimmery! Oh, and maybe we can still make sandcastles, but out of graham cracker crumbs, like the sand here!"

"That's perfect!" Amirah cheered. "If you just use your imagination, I bet your mermaid birthday party will be the best mermaid party ever!"

Olivia's face lit up with a huge smile. "I think you're right! And you know what? With the rain streaming down the windows, it will really feel like we're underwater!"

Amirah giggled. "I love it when everything works out!" she replied.

"Amirah! Olivia!"

Elvis's voice carried faintly across the sand. Despite the sound of the wind and the waves, the excitement in it was unmistakable.

"Do you think everything is okay?" Olivia asked as she and Amirah stood up.

"I think it's better than okay," Amirah said. "Come on—let's find out!"

The girls ran across the sand to join Elvis and Mei at a long table. It reminded Amirah of the birthday party table that they'd discovered in the woods—except this one was filled with brilliant colors, from the tablecloth to the bright balloons that bobbed overhead. There were four chairs and four place settings and—

"*Four* cakes?" Amirah gasped.

Elvis grinned at her. "It's a B-Bud Birthday Bash!" he exclaimed.

"My unicorn cake!" Amirah cried with glee. "It looks just like the one we made at home for my party!"

"Wow, you are a good baker!" Elvis murmured.

Amirah grinned. "There's a special surprise inside! Like a piñata!"

"What?" all three B-Buds asked at the same time.

"You'll see when I cut it." Amirah giggled.

"That looks exactly like the strawberry shortcake my oba-chan makes," Mei said, her eyes wide. "How is this even possible?"

"I've never had strawberry shortcake at a birthday party," Amirah commented. "But what a delicious idea!"

Mei nodded. "It's a popular birthday cake at home, in Japan. You can use any fruit you like, but strawberry is my favorite. It's also sort of a tradition in my family. My oba-chan has made one for my party every single year!"

"Tell us about your birthday cake," Amirah encouraged Olivia.

"It's this one here," Olivia said as she reached for a platter that was stacked with towers of triangles. "We call it fairy bread in Australia. It's not cake, exactly, but it's what we have for birthdays. You cut bread into triangles and spread some butter on it and then cover it—I mean absolutely cover it—with hundreds and thousands."

"Hundreds and thousands of what?" Elvis asked.

Olivia giggled. "That's what we call them in Australia," she explained. "You know. Because there are hundreds and thousands . . ."

As she took a closer look, Amirah's eyes widened. "Wait a minute. Are those *sprinkles?*" she exclaimed. "Fairy bread is covered in *sprinkles?*"

"Yes," Olivia replied. "Hundreds and thousands!"

"Hundreds and thousands," Amirah repeated. "I like the sound of that. Sprinkles are better when there are *hundreds* and *thousands* of them, after all!"

Elvis rubbed his hands together with anticipation. "I don't know if I'm more excited that my B-Buds get to have a piece of my peanut butter and banana birthday cake—or that *I* get to have a piece!" he joked.

"I think we all know the answer to that," Mei teased him.

As everyone laughed, a swirl of glitter swept over the table. When it disappeared, each special birthday dessert had a flickering candle on top!

"I think I know what this means," Amirah said, grinning. "Time for the birthday song!"

As the B-Buds sang the birthday song together, Amirah's heart filled with joy. When the last notes of the song drifted away on the ocean breeze, the B-Buds knew it was time to make their birthday wishes.

Amirah knew exactly what she wanted to wish for. She closed her eyes as she got ready to blow out her candle. Around the table, she could sense that the other B-Buds were doing the same. She took a deep breath and blew hard. When Amirah opened her eyes again, there was no flame on her candle. Just a plume of smoke twirling into the air.

"Remember, don't tell anyone what you wished for," Amirah said. "Otherwise, it won't come true."

Elvis was already cutting big slices of his peanut butter and banana cake and passing them around.

Amirah waited for Elvis to finish and then picked up a knife next to her special cake. "B-Buds! Watch this!" she cried.

Everyone gathered around as Amirah carefully sliced into the unicorn cake. When she lifted up the first piece, a waterfall of sprinkles—hundreds and thousands!—cascaded out of the cake, spilling over the table. As the B-Buds gasped in delight, Amirah beamed. The unicorn cake was as wonderful as she had imagined it would be!

AFTER THE B-BUDS shared their special birthday cakes, after they laughed themselves silly, after they played birthday games for hours on the sandy shore, the sun started to set. The sky was a swirl of cotton-candy colors: pink and blue and purple. Though the first stars hadn't appeared yet, Amirah had a sudden, surprising longing.

She wanted to go home.

Home to her family, home to her friends, home to her birthday party with everyone she loved.

"I didn't think I'd ever want to leave the Magical Land of Birthdays," she said. "But . . ."

"Me too," Mei said.

"My dad always plays the birthday song on his harmonica," Elvis said. "I'd hate to miss it."

Amirah smiled at him. Then she turned to Olivia. "What about you?" she asked.

Olivia nodded vigorously. "Yes! I've got to

158

hurry home!" she exclaimed. "There's so much to do for my party—crush up all those graham crackers to make sand, hang the streamers to look like seaweed, make my mermaid dress . . ."

"And make fairy bread with lots of hundreds and thousands," Amirah added.

"Of course. Can't forget the hundreds and thousands," Olivia said with a grin.

"I know we need to get back," Mei began. "But I'm really going to miss you all. You're my B-Buds!"

"We come from four different countries, spread all over the world," Elvis said. "How will we ever see each other again?"

Olivia's smile began to fade. "I don't want to say goodbye forever," she said. "I don't want this adventure to end."

"B-Buds! What are you talking about?" Amirah asked in disbelief. "This isn't the end! And it's definitely not goodbye forever. It's just . . . for now."

"How do you know for sure?" asked Elvis.

Amirah threw her arms out wide. "You don't think we'll be back?" she asked him. "After I visited the Magical Land of Birthdays in my dream, and spent the most special day of the year here—our birthday—with my B-Buds? I just *know* we'll be back!"

"That's no guarantee, though," Elvis replied.

"Here's *my* guarantee," Amirah said, thinking fast. She pulled the container of sprinkles out of her pocket. "Sprinkles—or hundreds and thousands—for everyone!"

"Why?" asked Mei.

"Because sprinkles are magic—just like this place," Amirah said. "Just like birthdays. Besides, they helped me get here today . . . and I have this funny feeling that they might help all of you too. Now, hold out your hands."

The B-Buds held out their palms. Amirah started with Mei and poured some sprinkles into her hand. Strangely, only purple sprinkles poured out of the vial.

"My favorite color!" Mei said, pleased.

"That's never happened before," Amirah said, staring at the container. Then she moved on to Elvis. When she shook the sprinkle vial, only green ones appeared in his hand.

"Let me guess," she began. "Green is your favorite color?"

"Right!" he replied.

Amirah laughed. "See what I mean?" she said as she turned to Olivia. "Sprinkles are magic!"

This time, when Amirah put sprinkles into Olivia's hands, only blue ones appeared.

"Magic," Olivia agreed.

"Birthday magic got us here," Amirah told the B-Buds. "And birthday magic will bring us back. I promise."

Her friends looked so relieved that Amirah smiled even bigger.

That's when she noticed something odd: a driftwood sign in the shape of an arrow. It had a single word carved on it: HOME.

"Was that there before?" Amirah asked, confused.

"I . . . don't think so," Mei replied. "But . . . maybe we just didn't notice it."

"Maybe," Amirah said—but she didn't sound convinced.

"How can one sign lead to home for all of us?" Elvis asked. "We couldn't live farther apart if we tried!"

"I don't know," Amirah said. "But I trust the Magical Land of Birthdays. It's always sent us in the right direction before."

When she started walking toward the sign, the other B-Buds joined her. They followed a series of driftwood arrows, chatting eagerly about all the birthday fun that would be waiting for them when they got home. When they reached the top of one of the taller dunes, Amirah stopped suddenly.

"Look," she said, pointing. "Is that it? Is that our way home?"

Down on the sand, there was a merry-go-round, with shiny silver poles and ribbon streamers that fluttered in the breeze. It had six sections: one purple, one blue, one green, one orange, one yellow, and one pink.

"Just like the colors of the rainbow," Amirah breathed.

"I bet we're supposed to hop on the section that's our favorite color," Mei said.

Amirah knew Mei was right and that the pink section was meant for her. But then she realized there were two extra sections on the merry-go-round. Who were the orange and yellow sections for?

"You three get on and hold on tight," Elvis told them. "I'll give us a big push."

"But how will you get home?" Olivia asked.

"Once it's spinning fast, I'll jump on," he replied. "Everyone ready?"

"Yes!" chorused Amirah, Mei, and Olivia.

"Then here we go!" Elvis said. He grabbed one of the poles and started to run. The merry-go-round moved slowly at first, but soon it started to pick up speed. Elvis's determined face turned red as he struggled to keep up.

"Come on, Elvis!" Mei called.

"Jump on—before it's too late!" Amirah added.

With one last burst of speed, Elvis leaped onto the merry-go-round and grasped the silver pole with both hands, landing on the green section. Amirah sighed in relief. Then she threw back her head and laughed with joy!

"Happy birthday, B-Buds!" Amirah shouted.

"Happy birthday!" she heard her B-Buds shout back.

The merry-go-round was spinning faster, faster, faster . . . The colors blurred into a swirling rainbow that shattered into so many pieces . . .

Hundreds and thousands, Amirah thought as everything grew so bright that finally, she had to shut her eyes.

When she opened them again, she was all alone.

And she was home.

CHAPTER THIRTEEN

"I'M BACK," Amirah whispered. "I'm back!"

She was in her bedroom. The curtains were closed; she couldn't tell if it was night or day. How much time had passed, exactly? Amirah tapped her temples as she tried to remember. She and Mama had just finished making her special cake . . . Amirah's Birthday Cake from *The Power of Sprinkles* . . .

I didn't miss it, did I? Amirah suddenly worried. What if she'd spent her *entire* birthday in the Magical Land of Birthdays?

Amirah sat up and rubbed her eyes. Her head felt a little fuzzy. Had it all been a dream? Had she slept through her entire birthday? What if it was over, and she'd have to wait a whole year for it to come again?

There was a knock at the door.

"Come in," Amirah said eagerly.

It was Mama. Amirah's rainbow-striped party dress was draped over her arm. "Ironed

and ready for you, princess!" Mama announced. "You'll have just enough time to get ready before the guests arrive."

"Thank you!" Amirah cried. "I can't wait for my birthday party!"

Mama smiled. "Neither can I," she replied as she raised the shades on the window and sunlight flooded into the room. "Everyone is going to *love* your special cake."

Amirah grinned back at her mother. "I can't wait for everyone to see the special surprise inside," she said. "All those hundreds and thousands!"

"Hundreds and thousands?" Mama asked.

"Oh—that's what they call sprinkles in Australia," Amirah explained. "Speaking of sprinkles, I need a refill. My container is emp . . ."

As Amirah took her sprinkle stash out of her pocket, though, her voice trailed off.

It was filled to the brim.

A little magic from the Magical Land of Birthdays, she thought as she returned it to her pocket.

"That reminds me," Mama said. "I have a little present for you. I wanted to give it to you now, before everyone gets here . . ."

Mama's eyes were twinkling as she held out a golden box tied with a big bow.

"Oooh, my first birthday present!" Amirah said. "Thank you, Mama! What is it?"

"Open it and find out," Mama replied.

Amirah perched on the end of her bed and carefully untied the bow. When she lifted the lid of the box, Amirah was left speechless by the special gift nestled in the tissue paper.

"Oh, Mama," she finally whispered.

Amirah reached into the box and pulled out the most gorgeous tiara she'd ever seen. It was covered with tiny crystals that glittered as they caught the light, casting rainbows around

the room like so many sprinkles. It was the very center of the tiara, though, that left Amirah too stunned to speak. A unicorn made of gemstones—the mirror image of Cara, right down to the golden horn and rainbow mane—was the centerpiece. Amirah stared at it and remembered, in dazzling detail, every moment of her incredible adventure in the Magical Land of Birthdays. When she had first woken up, she was almost sure it had only been a dream, but now she felt just as sure it wasn't. And then another thought popped into her head. *Did Mama know about the Magical Land of Birthdays and Cara the Unicorn?*

"I know it's different than all of your other birthday tiaras," Mama said. "But it just seemed so perfect for you—perfect in every way—magical, even . . ."

Amirah looked up fast. "Did you say *magical?* How did you know?" she asked, tracing her finger across the unicorn's sparkly gems.

170

"Know what?" Mama asked.

"That I would love it," Amirah replied.

Smiling warmly, Mama reached over and pulled Amirah into a hug. "I just had a feeling, princess. I'm glad I was right."

As Amirah hugged her mother back, she still wasn't sure if she really did know about Cara the Unicorn or not. If Mama did know about Cara—if she knew about the Magical Land of Birthdays—if she knew the truth about *The Power of Sprinkles*—

"Here," Mama said. "Let me help you put it on."

Amirah sat very still as Mama smoothed back her curls. Then Mama carefully positioned the tiara on Amirah's head. It was not as heavy as she expected. Instead, the beautiful tiara felt just right.

Amirah walked across the room to look in the mirror. As she moved, the tiara didn't budge, not even a fraction of an inch.

When she saw her reflection, Amirah couldn't help but smile. She knew she'd spend days—weeks—maybe even months—recalling the memories of her incredible adventures in the Magical Land of Birthdays with her B-Buds. She still had so many questions. There were still so many things that didn't make sense.

Then again, Amirah realized, maybe she didn't need to fully understand. Maybe that was part of what made it so special. After all, today was her birthday.

And birthdays are magic!

THE BIRTHDAY FUN ISN'T OVER!

Turn the page for baking tips and activities that will help you to keep living the birthday lifestyle!

BAKING TIPS FROM AMIRAH!

FOOD COLORING is a great way to create bright, beautiful colors for icing your cakes. But remember that less is more when it comes to food coloring! You can always add more color, but you can't take color away.

To create the perfect shade of blue frosting, start with just a few drops of blue food coloring in white icing and then stir to see how rich the color is, knowing you can always add more, one drop at a time, until you achieve the perfect color!

ICING is sticky, so you can use it like glue! Want to affix a unicorn horn made of an ice cream cone or some mouse ears

made out of cookies to the top of your cake? Icing works great. Not to mention that it tastes delicious!

SKETCH out your perfect cake before you decorate it so that you have a "map" to follow while decorating. This way, you can decide in advance where you want certain elements to go without having to worry about running out of room to complete your design.

 MEASURE CAREFULLY! Baking is a science, so you want to be exact and make sure to measure your ingredients precisely!

How many flavors of birthday cake have you tried? List them!

◇ ◆ ◇

_____

_____

_____

_____

_____

_____

_____

_____

_____

_____

_____

_____

_____

_____

_____

_____

_____

_____

Now list all the birthday cake flavors you would LIKE to try!

In the story, Olivia is planning a mermaid-themed birthday party, while Amirah's birthday party will have a unicorn theme. What are the best birthday party themes you can think of? List them!

From the best birthday party themes you listed on the previous page, choose your absolute favorite theme. Now imagine that you have to create your own birthday party with that theme. What decorations will you make? What foods will you serve? What else will you do to make your party special?

◇◆◇

_____

_____

_____

_____

_____

_____

_____

_____

_____

_____

_____

_____

_____

_____

What's your best birthday memory?
Write about it!

Now write about something you have done to make someone else's birthday special. It's okay if it hasn't happened yet—you can also use this space to plan a birthday surprise for someone special!

One of Amirah's favorite birthday traditions is the pancake breakfast her Baba makes for her. Do you have a favorite birthday tradition? Write about it! If not, write about a birthday tradition you would like to have!

In the story, Elvis is really good at playing music, and Mei is really good at gymnastics. What's the thing you are really good at? Write about it.

◇ ✧ ◇

_____

_____

_____

_____

_____

_____

_____

_____

_____

_____

_____

_____

_____

_____

_____

_____

Who are your B-Buds? Do you know anyone from school or your family who is a B-Bud? If not, ask your parent or caregiver to help you research online or at the library to find out who some of your famous B-Buds might be.
List their names here.

◆

What does your dream birthday cake look like? Draw a picture of it!

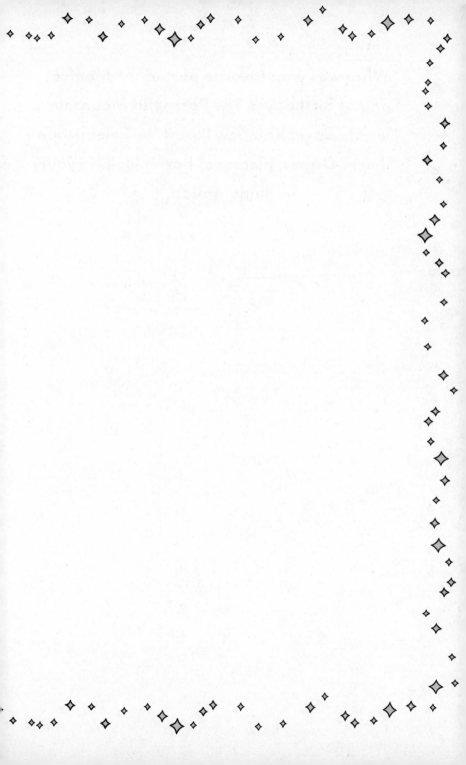

What was your favorite part of the Magical Land of Birthdays? The Party Hat Mountains, Candle Cave, Rainbow Forest, or Celebration Shore? Draw a picture of how it looks in your imagination.

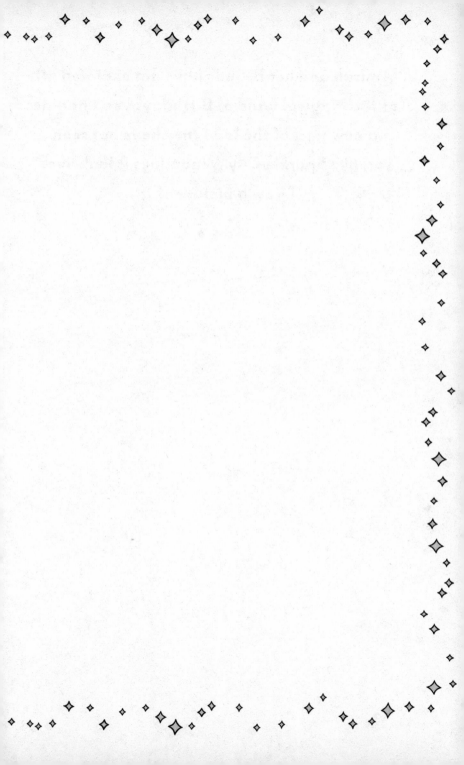

Amirah and her B-Buds have not explored all of the Magical Land of Birthdays yet. Imagine a new part of the land they have not seen yet, like Sparkle City. What does it look like? Draw a picture of it!

Flour Shop founder and Flour-ist Amirah Kassem is an artist at heart and cake is her medium. Amirah is the bestselling author of *The Power of Sprinkles*. Amirah grew up baking and sculpting with her mother in Mexico, where she discovered an appreciation for fine ingredients—and mastered the art of multisensory experiences.

THE ADVENTURE CONTINUES IN

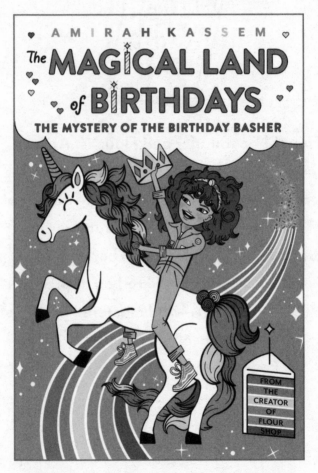

AMIRAH KASSEM

The MAGICAL LAND of BIRTHDAYS

THE MYSTERY OF THE BIRTHDAY BASHER

FROM THE CREATOR OF FLOUR SHOP

READ ON FOR A SNEAK PEEK!

BEFORE BED THAT NIGHT, Amirah reached for her favorite book. It wasn't a novel or a storybook, but a cookbook—a very special cookbook—that Mrs. Maria had given her six months ago: *The Power of Sprinkles*.

It was, Amirah suspected, the cookbook that had started it all.

That's where she had found a special birthday cake recipe with her name on it, which was a big surprise. Amirah loved her name, which meant "princess," but it was unusual enough that she rarely saw in print.

The Power of Sprinkles also had unique recipes for all her B-Buds' favorite birthday cakes. Amirah couldn't help smiling as she thought about Mei and Elvis and Olivia. But just as quickly, the memory of the empty shelves at the store came back to her, and

Amirah's smile started to fade. More than anything, she wished she could see her B-Buds and tell them about it.

To cheer herself up, Amirah started turning the pages of the old cookbook. No matter how gentle she was, some of the gold binding flaked off in her hands. That wasn't the most unusual thing about this book. The first time she had turned these pages, a cloud of sparkles that only Amirah could see had appeared, dancing and twinkling up her fingers, up her hand, up her arm—an early sign of the magic within.

That didn't happen much anymore, though, but Amirah wasn't worried. She knew the cookbook was just as powerful as ever.

It had been a busy day, but not just that—it had been a day of roller-coaster emotions. And the heat was so tiring. No wonder Amirah was exhausted, flipping through the cookbook in a dreamlike state as the crickets sang their night-time song outside her window.

Amirah covered her mouth as she yawned. She'd go to bed soon—she'd fall asleep, whether she wanted to or not—but not just yet. She still had to read over the recipe for Mei's birthday cake, a strawberry shortcake with sugar-syrup-soaked sponge cake that was practically bursting with juicy berries. Amirah licked her lips. As she read over the ingredients, she could almost taste them—sugar, cream, vanil—

Wait. The word . . . it was . . . it was fading . . . right before her eyes . . .

No . . . all the words . . . the entire recipe . . . disappearing . . .

"No!" Amirah cried, powerless to stop the recipe from vanishing. Frantically, she grabbed the page, as if her fingers could hold the words there before they disappeared for good.

And then, just like magic, they were back: each and every word, exactly as it had been before. Not a single letter out of place.

Amirah's heart was thudding in her chest

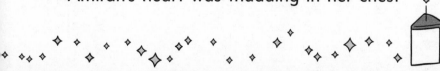

as she stared at the page. *That did* not *just happen,* she thought. *Printed recipes in cookbooks don't disappear. It's not possible. I must have dozed off . . . I was probably having one of those dreams where you don't know you're dreaming . . .*

But Amirah knew that she had been very much awake.

Gently—almost tenderly—she closed the cookbook and slid it under her pillow. She didn't want to be separated from *The Power of Sprinkles,* not after what had just happened—or what she thought had just happened.

As Amirah rested her head on her rainbow-striped pillowcase, she fell into a deep, restless sleep.

And this time, she dreamed.

IN HER DREAM, Amirah blinked—once, then twice—as a grin spread across her face. "I'm back," she whispered joyfully. "I'm back!"

The Magical Land of Birthdays stretched

all around her, as far as she could see. But as Amirah looked around, her smile began to fade. She was in the Magical Land of Birthdays again—there was no doubt about that—but it wasn't quite as enchanting as she remembered.

In fact, it wasn't very enchanting at all.

Amirah's nose wrinkled as she caught the scent of burned birthday cake drifting by on the breeze. She'd only smelled it once before, when an unexpected visitor prevented Mama from taking a cake out of the oven in time, but the harsh, charred smell was one she'd never forget.

A heavy mist—mixed with a tinge of smoke—hung over the land, making the once brilliant colors appear washed out and faded. The colorful cake pops lining the path made a sorry sight as their frosting oozed to the ground in fat, greasy droplets. Helium balloons in the sky began to droop, as if each one had sprung a leak at the exact same time. The streamers that decorated each tree had lost all

their festiveness, flopping from the branches as if they'd been caught in a bad storm.

A storm.

Just as the word popped into Amirah's head, a gust of smoky wind picked up. It whipped her hair around her face, and she quickly twisted it into a messy bun at the back of her head—just in time to see something: a faded scrap of paper carried on the wind.

Instinctively, Amirah wanted to know what it was.

It fluttered to the ground a few feet away, so Amirah left the path to pick it up. The soft green grass that she remembered growing in the Magical Land of Birthdays was dry and brittle now. It crunched under her feet and turned to powder with every step she took.

She approached the piece of paper cautiously.

Don't be so silly, Amirah told herself. *It's just a piece of paper. It can't hurt you.*

Soon she was close enough to see that there was something written on it. Could it be a message—a message for *her?* This wouldn't be the first time the Magical Land of Birthdays had tried to tell her something.

Something told Amirah that it was important. But still, for some reason, she hesitated. Just as Amirah reached out her hand—

Whoosh!

Another sudden gust of wind picked up the paper and carried it farther away!

Amirah frowned. Now she was determined—completely and utterly determined—to read whatever was written on the paper. She didn't dawdle this time. Instead, Amirah scrambled over the rocky hillside. Soon she was close enough to see the word BIRTHDAY written on the paper in bold, blocky handwriting. She reached out again and—

Whoosh!

This is getting ridiculous, Amirah thought

as, once again, the paper fluttered just out of reach, landing in the crook of a wizened old tree. She raced the wind to reach it, hoping against hope that the tree's rough bark would somehow keep it there until she could reach it. The wind was blowing harder now. It almost seemed to be pushing her forward, faster, faster, faster—until suddenly, there she was, standing in the shadow of the gnarled tree.

The snippet of paper, still stuck in the tree, was just out of her reach.

Amirah took a deep breath, crouched down low, and leaped into the air. Her fingers brushed the edge of the paper. She grabbed and grasped and closed her hand around it in a tight fist. Amirah didn't trust that wind, with its eerie mist and stench of smoke. She wouldn't let it take the paper away from her again.

Amirah was so eager to see what the paper had to say that her hands trembled a little as she unfolded it.

"An invitation!" she exclaimed, speaking aloud even though there was no one to hear her. It was in pretty bad shape, though. The bottom half of the birthday party invitation was missing, and it almost looked like it had been clawed or shredded. The color was faded to a muted, splotchy grayish-red. She couldn't tell whose party it was, or where it was supposed to be held. Besides the heading, which read YOU'RE INVITED TO A BIRTHDAY PARTY!, the only other part Amirah could read was the date—July 8, almost exactly one year ago.

Maybe that was why the invitation was in such bad shape. The party had happened a long time ago.

Or, Amirah thought, maybe there was another reason.

Just like that, the invitation—or what was left of it—crumbled into sparkly dust in her hands.

"No!" Amirah cried. But it was too late.

The invitation was gone.

She sighed heavily and looked around the empty landscape. That was when she realized the most unusual thing about the Magical Land of Birthdays: the silence. There was no laughter, no music, no happy birthday song. Just empty, hollow silence that blanketed the land as thoroughly as the mist.

Amirah decided to climb the rest of the way up the hillside. It wasn't very far. She hoped, at the top of the hill, she might be able to see more of her favorite place. Maybe she'd even be able to figure out where that burned smell was coming from.

At the top of the hill, Amirah finally realized where she was. It was an area of the Magical Land of Birthdays that she'd never visited before—but she'd seen it on a map, and knew she'd never forget it.

Sparkle City.

With the smoky mist growing thicker by the minute, Amirah didn't want to ven-

ture into that unfamiliar city all alone. She wished—and not for the first time—that her B-Buds were with her.

Then, in a flash of inspiration, she suddenly realized that she wouldn't have to go alone. Cara the Unicorn lived in the Magical Land of Birthdays! Amirah and Cara had shared a special bond from the moment they met, when Cara was stuck in piñata form and Amirah had freed her. They'd traveled the length of the Magical Land of Birthdays and back again. No matter what, Amirah knew, Cara would always come when Amirah needed her.

"Cara!" Amirah's voice echoed off the buildings as if the city were calling for Cara too. "Cara!"

Amirah didn't just listen for hoofbeats; she pressed her palms against the ground, hoping to feel it vibrating as Cara's golden hooves thundered across the land. But the

silence stretched on. Amirah called for Cara again and again, but there was no sign that the unicorn heard her.

Amirah stood up, wrapped her arms around herself, and shivered—even though the day wasn't particularly cold. There was no way for her to deny it any longer.

No one was coming.

Not her B-Buds.

Not even Cara.